The Road That Runs

Madame Verte

To Breda
I hope you enjoy This sequel
Cordialement
Madame Verte

For Tim

First Published 2017

First Edition

The Road that Runs

Preface

Madame Lapin has passed a restless night. She has tossed and turned and awoken frequently from oppressive dreams. She has drowned in rhubarb-infused olive oil. She has been smothered by peach jelly. She has fallen, Alice-like, down the inside of an endless jam jar. Now, peering through one unfocussed eye, she looks towards the slightly open window through which chilly gusts of wind have entered and alerted her to morning's arrival. They are blowing the overflowing contents of a make-do ashtray around the room. The little gusts are full of threat of bigger things to come: the first of the interminable November mistrals.

Despite this cold but fresh air, a familiar and unwanted scent permeates the room. What is that? Madame Lapin can't quite put her manicured finger on it. If she didn't know better, she might identify its source as onions. Then she begins to remember. She is filled with those emotions that are all too familiar to those who retire to bed having shared the evening with a quantity of red wine. The bed is shuddering under the noise of a distant rumble. Merde. Madame Lapin is an intellectual and an entrepreneur. She's a lady who likes to wake to the sound of the business news on the radio. A woman who, having updated herself with current affairs, might switch the channel to one that plays light classical music whilst she prepares the coffee.

Madame Lapin turns slowly in her noisy, smelly bed and is appalled to find a silver-haired, gold-chained, stubble infested man fast asleep with his mouth wide open. A plate of cold and congealed paella sits to his left patiently waiting for the hour of petit déjeuner. Putain. How did it come to this?

Part One

Chapter One

It's November again. Saturday. Monsieur Martin, busy with bales of hay for the small spotted ponies, and wrapped against the biting chill of the mistral, finds it difficult to believe another year has passed. Monsieur Martin, being a man of pragmatism, is not generally one for philosophical reflection. He treats each Provençal autumnal day as it appears. Sometimes the sun shines gloriously as he awaits Christmastide. On rare occasions the land is drenched from torrential downpours as he considers another season's courgettes. Generally, it's just windy. And, as the days are so short, there's no opportunity for the children of Cabannes to practise their equine skills in the evenings. This means that the miniature riding school can only function on a Saturday.

This year, however, things are a little different. Apart from the ever constant companionship of Clovis the wolf-dog, Monsieur Martin is alone at his work. Last year, he had Gerard to calm the ponies who are startled by the capricious wind. Gerard, the horse whisperer, would recount the old folk tales of Provence in soothing tones that made the small spotted ponies feel secure. This year, they are disturbed by the roughness of the mistral which noisily bends the branches of the remaining pear trees. Gerard has returned to the South with his reclaimed father, where his once distraught mother was waiting with open arms. And quite right too thinks Monsieur Martin magnanimously. But, all the same, he could do with an extra pair of hands.

Monsieur Martin looks across the fence that divides his land from that of his neighbours. He is searching for the comfort of continuity even though he knows his friend, the partner who cannot be named, is unlikely to be lounging in his Swedish garden chair. However, Monsieur Martin has the ghost of a sense that, above the howl of the mistral, he can hear faint sounds of Bulgarian jazz. This must be an aberration. This must be nothing more than a subliminal desire. But Monsieur Martin spots an abject figure roaming beyond the raised vegetable and flower beds.

The abject figure is dressed in an eclectic range of clothing. In fact, the partner who cannot be named is currently wearing almost all the clothes he possesses. This is the problem with Provence: most of the time, clothes are unnecessary. In the summer months, Monsieur Martin, as we know, passes his days in a state of semi-undress. The partner who cannot be named, being an intellectual, would never go this far. Nonetheless, if he has a shirt and trousers attached to his body, who cares whether either or both are fastened? He certainly doesn't. It's a different can of worms once the mistral kicks in. It's the kind of can from which one might select an especially fat specimen that advises you to wrap up well.

Monsieur Martin and the partner who cannot be named are united in their mutual delight at meeting each other. They exchange Bonjours. They trade condolences regarding the weather. They each ignore what the other is wearing because it occurs to neither to notice; let alone articulate what might be glaringly obvious to an outsider. A million miles apart culturally, they are, nonetheless conjoined by gender and place. They talk about their significant others.

For the partner who cannot be named, this means Phyllida. To most folk, Phyllida is the consummate hostess during the summer. In the winter months, once the needs and desires of the Norwegian Blues have been attended to, there is not much to occupy her time. This year, however, Phyllida has a project. Motivated by the gift of a rejected dishwasher from Mas Saint Antoine, Phyllida has decided to purchase a new kitchen. Which means that, in the face of limited finances, Phyllida and the partner will install the new kitchen. A few Bulgarians may be providing a musical accompaniment. The kitchen, like most items that are purchased on their side of the fence, will come from a Swedish catalogue. And like most items that come from the Swedish catalogue, the kitchen, in all its various parts, is still in a warehouse built for the purpose of housing items from Swedish catalogues.

This doesn't, of course, mean that preparations cannot commence. In fact, preparations began some weeks ago when the rejected dishwasher from Mas Saint Antoine was wheeled on a sack truck along the road between Noves and Cabannes. The receiving kitchen, being tiny, rural and French in nature, did not offer an obvious location for the rejected dishwasher. Accoutrements that had sat comfortably within for some years had to be removed in order to create a space. Actually, the kitchen had to be redesigned to specific specifications in order that the rejected dishwasher could be successfully squeezed into a suitable slot for the plumbing business. This was overseen by Phyllida, Louise who had rejected the dishwasher in the first place, a nameless entity from Cabannes who happened to be passing on his tractor and four felines of the Norwegian Blue variety.

At the time, the partner who cannot be named was missing in action. Or, in his case, in non-action. The partner has never made it a priority to venture in the direction of the kitchen and the arrival of a rejected dishwasher was no excuse to change the habits of a Provençal lifetime. However, in other lifetimes, passed in other incarnations in other countries, the partner had proved surprisingly adept at renovations. Phyllida knows this because, over the years, she has made it her duty to interrogate thoroughly any previous wives or suchlike should they raise their heads above the parapet that guards the fortress of the past.

The partner, who may be litigious in nature, is very well aware of this. He knows he will eventually have to find his way to the kitchen and activate his practical abilities in the tiling and grouting departments. Nonetheless, as he informs Monsieur Martin, when women are in supervising mode, it's best to keep clear. Therefore, when Phyllida, Louise and the unknown tractor driver were installing the dishwasher, the partner was busy doing nothing in his jungle garden behind the house. And when the rejected dishwasher was finally plumbed in and switched on, which was about the same time as various shrieks and shouts blocked out the musical Bulgarians, and screeching wet cats were seen fleeing in all directions, the partner who cannot be named decided the best option would be to stand silently behind a large fig tree.

Monsieur Martin and Clovis, on hearing this account, nod sympathetically and one of them utters the only possible response: 'meh bah.'

Chapter Two

Over in Graveson, Jack Shaker, frequent visitor to the Bar-Tabac at St Remy, is hot, tired and upset. In the summer, Jack is often hot and tired. Some years ago, he moved from Wiltshire to Provence because he believed the climate would be better for his health. In general, the climate *is* better: the sky lacks the greyness of England and his health is reasonable. If it wasn't for the heat, life would be great. It's not the summer now. It's November and with the best will in the world you couldn't say it was hot. In fact, the icy wind of the mistral is far colder than the mild English autumn Jack has seen accounts of on his satellite induced BBC. Jack is tired and upset because he can't sleep. He can't sleep because the bloody wind howls above and around him from bedtime until breakfast.

Last night, he finally gave way to the elements and to all thoughts of sleep. If you're an ex-pat in Provence, you can do this. You don't have to get up for work in the morning. People like Jack have spent most of their adult lives getting up for work in the morning. That's how they can afford to live quietly in Provence. Except that it's not quiet. It's windy. Around two in the morning, Jack clambered out of his bed, went downstairs and put the television on. Jack watched the test match with his fox terrier, Buddy. England versus the West Indies. The West Indies don't have a very good side this year. England appeared to have submitted their badminton team. They were thrashed by the West Indies. Buddy slept peacefully. He's not keen on cricket. Jack shouted at the England team. The television commentator, Kevin, shouted at the England selectors. The England selectors ignored Kevin and the England cricket team ignored Jack. That's why Jack is tired and cross. It doesn't explain, however, why, in the middle of November, Jack is hot.

When Jack had finished shouting at the English cricket team he thought he and Buddy might as well have an early breakfast. They each had a bowl of cornflakes and two pieces of toast. Jack wished he hadn't invited his friends and neighbours to dinner later in the day: he was so tired. Still, he had no good reason to put them off so he retrieved his piece of pork from the fridge and put it on a plate on the kitchen table to acclimatise. Of course, he wouldn't have been able to do this in the heat of high summer. In November, however, it's safe. Jack washed up the cereal bowls and the toast plates. Then he went back to bed to catch up on the missing sleep.

Buddy had watched Jack carefully whilst the housekeeping was undertaken. Buddy knew that when Jack had finished tidying up, they would go for a walk. Sometimes, Jack would put Buddy in the car and they would drive up to La Montagnette. Jack would stretch his legs and Buddy would run joyfully in circles looking for rabbits. It was too windy for La Montagnette today so Buddy anticipated a trot round the village which was full of wonderful French doggy smells. When Jack headed back to the bedroom, Buddy was confused. When Jack got back into bed, Buddy started barking. Buddy was trying to be helpful. He was reminding Jack that he'd forgotten the walk. Jack wasn't very polite to his dog. Buddy lay down for ten minutes. Then he got bored.

A couple of hours later, Jack gets up again. He has a shower and feels suitably refreshed. He doesn't feel at all hot. Yet. Jack wanders into the kitchen where one or two items appear to be missing. One of these is Buddy. The other is the piece of pork. Jack looks out of the window and spots both the missing items in close proximity to each other. In fact, one is in the mouth of the other. Given that the pork was well and truly dead when last seen, it isn't difficult, reader, to work out whose mouth is currently jammed with pig. Jack is furious and rushes out into the garden.

Buddy is thrilled that Jack has arrived for a game of chase. He immediately forgives Jack for forgetting the walk and rushes back and forth between the semi-ornate pillar that supports one end of the French veranda and the wooden post that holds the English bird table in place. Folk of many nationalities have sat on that veranda since Jack came to Provence. No birds of any nationality have ever sat on that bird table since Buddy arrived chez Shaker. Back and forth, from pillar to post, Buddy runs with Jack Shaker in hot-and-getting-hotter pursuit. Jack Shaker scores more runs than the England cricket team could imagine in their wildest dreams. Jack Shaker scores as many catches as the England cricket team. Which is to say, none. But, when he finally gives in and sits on his veranda with a large glass of something, hot, tired and upset, Jack has his eureka moment.

Jack Shaker has lived in Provence for the last ten years. He hasn't yet quite got the hang of the language. To be honest, he hasn't really got further than 'oui' or 'non.' However, unlike many ex-pats, Jack has somehow accumulated a huge number of friends of diverse nationalities and linguistic competencies. Tonight, for example, he's entertaining Cathy and Serge who are his French neighbours, a Dutch couple named Louise and Ruud, and their neighbours, Phyllida and the partner who cannot be named. As a result of three phone conversations, precipitated by news of the lost pork, Cathy, Louise and Phyllida have brought supper with them. It's a cosmopolitan crowd and a mixed variety of food. Fusion.

Apart from the olives and crisps, they haven't reached anything vaguely resembling food yet. However, there is one component of a meal in Provence that everyone, regardless of country of origin, embraces: shut in the dining room, with the blinds drawn against the windy elements, this party are enjoying the aperitif. And Jack is sharing an idea. Born of the carnage shared at previous quiz nights, and inspired by today's pillar to post nonsense, Jack has decided that the way to forge meaningful relationships in the local community is to organise an international cricket match. The ensuing silence at the table is broken by the partner who cannot be named, momentarily choking on an olive stone. 'Are there many rules in cricket?', he asks.

Chapter Three

Madame Martin is prowling around the kitchen muttering to herself. The Provençal markets are not merely a seasonal treat for transient tourists: they continue year round. Let's face it, bills also have to be paid in the winter months and anyway, the markets existed as a central point of commerce long before the travelling classes stumbled into the area. Nonetheless, it would be disingenuous to claim that there are quite as many customers demanding certain goods in November as there are during the crush of August, so Madame Martin has some respite. Which is just as well.

For a start, Madame Martin is sick to her tiny back teeth with the kitchen chez elle. It's hardly appropriate for jam and pickle production which, since originating at the domestic end of a scale previously unknown to exist, has escalated to somewhere that involves most of the baguettes in the South. Further, as with all expanding businesses, there's a problem with the staff. Netty and Sophie are good girls and have long since ceased hostilities. Of course, the problem with people that not only stop hating each other, but also become the best of friends, is that they have to have someone else at whom to vent the occasional frustrations that are thrown in the path of life. They aren't intentionally troublesome; neither are they particularly reliable. And talking of troublesome…

… Only yesterday, Madame Martin was over at the market in Eygalières with her jam, her pickle and her partner, Madame Lapin. That Madame Lapin actually made an appearance was a cause for celebration. If you thought those two young women were top of the pops in the department of flaky, you clearly haven't seen Madame Lapin since last summer's annual fête. And neither have many other folk. Here is a woman who has gone from hirsute feminist intellectual, to challenging entrepreneur, to shaved legged shadow of her former self. Here's a woman who's discovered men. And, loath though I am, reader, to mention the word, sex. And worse than sex, onions. Madame Lapin is head over very high heels in lust with that troublemaker from Orange, the infamous paella purveyor, Jean-Pierre Lucard.

The trouble with being in lust is that, largely, Madame Lapin doesn't really like Jean-Pierre Lucard. It's true that when she hears the engine of his trike approaching her bijou apartment in Cabannes, her knees begin to quiver. And every time she sees that unbuttoned pale blue shirt, all literary thoughts and entrepreneurial considerations of pickle are instantly abandoned. The foundations of Madame Lapin's world have become based on anticipation and promise. But, there's no getting away from it, the golden chain around her lover's neck is a tarnished irritant. The constant sweeping of discarded cigarette butts is a thorn in her sensual garden. She is heartily sick of re-heated paella suppers. And the over-riding smell of onions that permeates her life is superseded in the field of nausea only by the ever present competition from women who live within a six mile radius. These days, Madame Lapin finds it difficult to concentrate on anything other than this man who stands for everything she's always hated.

Madame Martin is sufficiently astute to realise her business partner has a problem. On one of her tiny hands, Madame Martin feels that what goes round comes round. Let's face it: one minute the jam queen had little in her life – the next, she had a small veterinary locum. Then Madame Lapin, who, allegedly, had no apparent interest in men, stole Monsieur Villiers along with many of Madame Martin's hopes and dreams. And no sooner had the only point of interest in Plan d'Orgon, apart from the memorial to the local and national hero, Jean Moulin, been snatched from her miniscule palms, than Madame Lapin discarded the tiny vet and moved on to that cheapskate from Orange. And a paella pan brimming with problems. Serve her right.

Alternatively, and on the matching tiny hand, Madame Martin has, as we know, eventually recognised the worth of her husband. She could also do with Madame Lapin regaining her position as professional business partner. In fact, Madame Martin could do with anyone, preferably female, to offer a bit of support.

There's a knock at the door.

I know what you're thinking reader. This door knocking business is in danger of becoming an overcooked literary cliché. But there's not much in the way of alternatives when you live down the end of a dusty lane that runs from the road between Noves and Cabannes in a house with no front door bell. In any case, it could be Monsieur Villiers returning to claim another role in Madame Martin's life and causing all sorts of fresh disturbance. Or it could be the paella purveyor whose twinkling eyes were originally pointed in the direction of Madame Martin at the annual fête. Conversely, it might simply be Madame Lapin arriving to discuss further nuances to the soon-to-be-expanding website. Madame Martin has no interest in any of these options. When the second knock is heard, she opens the door with far from French finesse. She finds Myrtle Meades, a woman devoid of concern for either jam or pickle.

Chapter Four

Monsieur Martin has fallen silent. He has listened with interest to the disturbing tale of the rejected dishwasher and the imminent renovations to his neighbours' kitchen and his anxiety levels have soared. This is all a little too close to home for his liking. Monsieur Martin knows only too well about women who begin by muttering in kitchens. He is well aware that mutters evolve into grumbles which quickly become suggestions. And suggestions have barely surfaced before the pleading commences; whilst pleading is almost immediately forgotten as demands are voiced. And we all know that demands are pointless if not accompanied by threats. Although he is only at the grumbling stage along the road to domestic upheaval, Monsieur Martin is about to share his own worries with the partner who cannot be named when he suddenly hears his wife calling.

Superbly synchronised, Monsieur Martin and Clovis turn from the fence that divides their land from that of the neighbours and see Madame Martin plodding towards them with her apron flapping in the wind. At some other point in time, Monsieur Martin may have turned in a similar way to consider the diminutive lady with her auburn locks flowing delightfully in the slightly-more-than a breeze. Actually, that may have been quite some time ago. Or in a dream. Anyway, today it's flapping aprons and something more distracting. Madame Martin is accompanied by a very tall woman unknown to Monsieur Martin. The very tall woman is dressed in rubber boots, baggy jeans, an indescribable jacket which seems to be wrapped over a number of thick jumpers and a woolly hat pulled over her ears. Merde, not another bloody feminist. And just as he's coming to terms with his analysis of the towering apparition, Monsieur Martin has an even more distressing thought: what if she's some sort of avant-garde kitchen designer!

The tall and the short arrive at the fence which separates French kitchens in some sort of disorder. Clovis, hitherto a silent bystander, practises a newly developed snarl in the direction of the tallest person in the gathering. The tallest person returns what can only be described as a silent and withering snarl of her own making. Clovis, somewhat surprisingly, appears to capitulate and slinks off into the pear trees. Madame Martin and the partner who cannot be named exchange Bonjours. Monsieur Martin stands aside with his hands behind his back, hiding the fact that several of his fingers are crossed. He is twitching and pulling strange faces at the partner. This is coded language in which he silently begs his neighbour not to mention dishwashers again. The partner who cannot be named regards Monsieur Martin with some alarm. He looks at the tall person who seems to be wearing even more clothes than he is. He makes a mental note that Madame Martin, currently trying to regain control of the badly behaved apron, doesn't appear in the best of moods. The partner has had more than enough recently of women who are not in the best of moods. He mumbles something incoherent about Bulgarians and politely takes his leave. Monsieur Martin looks at his wife and waits for an explanation.

Myrtle Meades and her husband, Richard, live in Noves. They are newcomers, having only moved over from England a couple of months ago. Noves is an up and coming extension of the ex-pat golden triangle. Locals have been pretty much priced out of St Remy by the once travelling-but-now-settling classes. As Plan d'Orgon is a non-starter in the home-and-away mentality, it's been necessary for new ex-pats to look in the other direction. Myrtle and Richard Meades were tipped the nod to Noves by their friend, Charlie O'Connor, he of cheesy chips fame. Richard was something to do with racing cars in a former incarnation. Details are irrelevant: what matters is that in her previous life, Myrtle Meades, who was tired of being a lady who lunches, became a volunteer in a home for abandoned and ill-treated ponies. And Myrtle Meades, having already refurbished her new Provençal homestead, is looking for further equine action.

As yet, Madame Martin knows nothing of Myrtle's provenance and currently cares even less. Like you, dear reader, Madame Martin had thought that the knock at the door might have been conveniently caused by someone with culinary skills and a spot of spare time. Her initial conversation with Myrtle had been tiresome on many levels. For a start, Madame Martin speaks little English beyond that which is necessary in order to explain the contents of various jars. Myrtle Meades, however, has a reasonable grasp of French and was able to convey her interest in the small spotted ponies. 'Meh bah', thinks Madame Martin. Anything that helps Monsieur Martin can only be good for lowering his anxiety levels. And a calm husband is likely to be far more amenable to potential kitchen improvements than one who is tired and worried.

Madame Martin introduces Myrtle Meades to Monsieur Martin. Madame Martin does her very best to contextualise the appearance of Myrtle Meades. Monsieur Martin doesn't really understand. Further, he is somewhat in awe of the ill-dressed woman who is soaring above him. Conversely, he notices that the small spotted ponies, who, only moments ago were shaking in the fearsome mistral, have gathered silently around the stranger in the woolly hat as if she was the source of newly found comfort. Disinclined as he is to mention the kitchen, Monsieur Martin suggests that the three of them adjourn to that place in order to continue discussions over a glass of something warming away from the wind.

It's a tricky interview. The language barrier is not helpful. The unexpected appearance of Christophe is more than a hindrance, particularly as the son and heir seems to find the guest hilarious. Nonetheless, at the end of an hour which Madame Martin feels could have been spent more productively, her husband has reached a number of conclusions. In no particular order these are: Myrtle Meades has experience and empathy with ponies; Myrtle Meades is not looking for a live-in position; Myrtle Meades is a volunteer. This last proves the most difficult for the Martins to comprehend. They have no experience of volunteering. The concept is a cultural step too far. However, once their tall guest manages to convince them that she is not looking for payment, Monsieur Martin reaches a decision. He offers Myrtle Meades the job as a replacement for Gerard. Under the table, Clovis whines.

Chapter Five

Down at the PMU bar in Cabannes a few days later, Christophe receives a strange phone call from Monsieur le patron of the Bar-Tabac des Alpilles at St Remy. The call is odd for a number of reasons. Firstly, Monsieur doesn't have the number of Christophe's phone and only calls the PMU bar on the off chance that the legendary academic and organiser of international quizzes might be in situ. Actually, it's not really strange that Christophe is propping up the bar on a Tuesday evening. Or any other evening come to that. It would be stranger if Christophe had been elsewhere. Moreover, the fact that Monsieur doesn't have the potato-packer's private number further indicates that there's still more than geographical distance between the two correspondents.

The subject of the telephone conversation is, to Christophe's mind, très bizarre. Monsieur le patron wants to know how much Christophe understands about the rules of cricket. Merde. Christophe is reluctant to admit that there are some things in life most folk know nothing about even if they aren't French, but he understands it's pointless to make things up; especially about cricket. Might as soon speak in Urdu. 'What's this now', he explodes, 'the bloody British Empire?' Monsieur le patron recognises this response. It's the same as he offered when the idea was posited by Jack Shaker earlier in the day over a glass of something or other in St Remy. Mon Dieu. Cheesy chips was an alien step too far; a mini-bus to Cabannes was a geographical nightmare. Culture is culture and territory is sacred. Cricket! Putain.

Monsieur le patron might not have even bothered to telephone that imbecile in Cabannes, but he'd had a secondary thought. Both rounds of the quiz had turned out to be an internecine affair: Cabannes versus St Remy. Some means of gaining superiority over those ex-pats would be a much better outcome. He does his best to persuade Christophe in this line of thought. And even though neither have the slightest idea what they're talking about, they somehow reach a conclusion that the world will never improve unless a cricket match has taken place. The rules are irrelevant. Can't be that difficult surely. The most important thing to agree on is the venue. The most difficult thing to agree on is the venue. There is nothing in the local vicinity that remotely corresponds to a cricket pitch. One chain plus three stumps are essential says Monsieur le patron. Reader, your narrator is unable to translate the response.

Monsieur le patron and Christophe reach agreement at the same time: it would be admitting premature defeat to ask an Englishman. They'll question the partner who cannot be named and who knows everything. Of course, the partner cannot be expected to visit either the PMU bar or the Bar-Tabac at St Remy. The two conspirators will make their way down the road that runs between Noves and Cabannes and call at Phyllida's place for a spot of liquid refreshment and a gathering of cricket related information.

. . . .

At some point in time, Monsieur le patron extricates himself from the enforced bonhomie of the PMU bar at Cabannes and, along with Christophe, travels out of that village in the direction of Noves. A number of alcoholic infused refreshments are already secured under their respective belts. Belts that have no intention of holding as much in place as that which commandeers the legendary blue jeans of Jean-Pierre Lucard. News of the intended cricket match, although unplanned and unintended, has already leaked into the environs. The idea was, initially, met with guffaws of laughter and disdain. However, as with many innovative ideas, particularly those that originate in the seat of government, the greater the intake of Pastis and the riper the conversation, the less a means of ensuring French superiority doesn't seem quite as bizarre. The missing-in-action paella purveyor has already been provisionally booked for the cricket dinner and the two intrepid cultural pioneers have been waved off with much enthusiasm as if on a destination-unknown safari trek.

The partner who cannot be named is grazing quietly in the Savannah of his newest garden unaware that explorers may be on their way. Sick to his back teeth of the on-off mistral, the partner has been extremely industrious. He has investigated hedging and ditching on l'internet. In this, he inexplicably arrived at the website of the Museum of English Rural Life. Quite how this happened will remain one of rural or urban life's conspiracies. It's of no consequence: the partner has woven bamboo along with some of the more pliable pear tree branches and is now prostrate on his Swedish garden chaise longue within a circular windbreak of mixed provenance. Bodies clothed in blue Norwegian blue fur have, uninvited, curled themselves around the partner. He cares little. He has succeeded in alienating himself totally from any of that ongoing nonsense in the kitchen and from life in general. Or so he believes. The partner who cannot be named might, in the worst case scenario, anticipate an intrusion from Phyllida. He might even be prepared for the Bulgarian musical interlude to be interrupted by French winds interfering with electrical connections. The last thing he expects is a couple of half-drunk French lads demanding explanations regarding the rules of cricket.

They arrive noisily and without warning. And as a visitation of sorts has taken place, Phyllida, finding a familiar role, insists on leading Christophe and Monsieur le patron, through a number of gates, past the raised, but now empty flower and vegetable plots, under a newly erected wooden arch and into the supposedly secret hiding place that the partner has constructed. Fortuitously, she has managed this without the aid of a map but with a selection of liquid refreshments to hand. The partner, increasingly of a litigious nature is horrified. As he recalls, the last time he entertained that imbecile from down the lane there was some sort of incident with the Swedish chaise longue. Still, it's Provence so there should be handshakes, jollity and continuous well-being. Mediaeval English poets must be temporarily discarded amongst the more resilient winter weeds.

It's difficult for the partner to sustain the bonhomie once the purpose of the visit has been established. Largely, this is because, in the face of cricket, it's even more difficult for him to continue playing the part of the man who knows everything. All is not lost, however. On the way to hedging and ditching, via the Museum of English Rural Life, the partner made an unanticipated incursion into the highlighted rules of village cricket from which he immediately surfed his way out.

'You'll have to give me time to ascertain all the details', he informs his visitors, wondering whether he will be able to relocate the relevant site. 'In the interim, however', he continues, 'I'm sure you know that the most important thing to accomplish is an acceptable after-match tea. Scones, sandwiches, cake and suchlike. It's not cricket otherwise'. A strange vision of an unbuttoned pale blue shirt, a golden medallion and a selection of delicately sliced gateaux is instantly banished from the mind of one of the French explorers the minute it raises its unrequested silver-haired head.

Chapter Six

When the small children of Cabannes arrive at the end of the lane for their riding lessons the following Saturday, a surprise awaits them. To be truthful, it isn't, at first, an altogether pleasant surprise; especially for the innocents in this saga. Since the departure of Gerard, the parents of the small children have become rather wary regarding the continued efficacy, efficiency and financial worth of the miniature riding school. It isn't that they doubt Monsieur Martin's equine abilities or his passion, particularly after his success at the annual fête: it's his ability to deal alone with eight small children that's in doubt. Monsieur Martin is unaware that he's on a probationary period. The invisible clock of which he has no knowledge has been ticking silently for some time.

The children rush into the paddock with Clovis simultaneously snarling and whimpering at their feet. Clovis, despite being an old hand, still doesn't know what to do in situations where so many tiny legs and feet are involved. On one paw, he's delighted to see all these visitors; on the other, he feels he has some sort of duty to advertise himself as a protective presence. The small spotted ponies are not so troubled. They spend far too much time wandering aimlessly in and out of the remaining pear trees. They appreciate that a great deal of life in Provence is considered unauthentic unless it's aimless but they are bored and long for the tiny folk who know them by name and encourage them over the little jumps.

Monsieur Martin has, of course, persuaded the children of Cabannes to recognise their mounts: Georges, Cabut, Maris, Tignous, Charb, Hebdo, Honore and Elsa. But today, there is another unknown presence in the paddock. The unknown presence looms in many senses. And the unknown presence is not immediately attractive to the small people owing to her immense height. The little children of Cabannes are tremulous. They nervously entwine their tiny fingers through the unruly manes of the ponies, as if attaching themselves bodily to their equine friends will afford some protection against the unexpected and unexpectedly tall personage.

Monsieur Martin has little experience in dealing with mass infantile hysteria. He tries to introduce Myrtle Meades to the miniature assembly but succeeds in doing nothing to instil calm and confidence. Myrtle Meades smiles. This is an unfortunate move that only makes matters worse as the smile of Myrtle Meades is not one of that lady's better features. It's the ponies, however, that save the day. Georges, Cabut, Maris and all the others, regardless of gender, have fallen in love with the tall apparition. They move joyously towards her with their mane clutching extensions in tow. And as the unconditional trust that the ponies have placed in Myrtle Meades gradually filters down that coarse hair and through the tiny fingers of the little children, there is an unheard but evident sigh as the paddock relaxes. Relief floods over Monsieur Martin like a Provençal tsunami.

During the past week, Myrtle Meades has been a regular visitor chez Martin in an effort to acclimatise to and empathise with her new working environment. Madame Martin wants nothing to do with this type of distraction and has made it clear that Myrtle can easily park her car where the lane ends and make her own way round the house and into the paddock without traipsing through a kitchen of embarrassments. It's bad enough having to run an expanding business in this squalor without being the source of ex-pat humour. In this, Madame Martin is mistaken. Myrtle Meades, being a woman who has been laughed at many times, does not laugh at others. Madame Martin has yet to discover this. Currently, however, she has little interest in women who have even less interest in jam and pickle.

Meanwhile, every time Monsieur Martin sees the apparition approaching, he visibly quakes in his mud-encrusted boots. He just can't seem to get used to the size of Myrtle Meades. Myrtle takes no notice of him. She's had a lifetime of folk taking a step backwards. Years of looking down on glamorous and appropriately sized, but inappropriately dressed, females draped over racing cars; years of dealing with her own neuroses: she's over it. And since Myrtle found chez Martin, she's never been happier.

There are no flashy motor cars and no ladies who lunch down this lane. There are no fashionistas and not too many judgements. No-one cares what she wears and her all pervasive contentment has spread about her environs and those within like a welcome dollop of peach jelly. Even so. It's still a shock to Monsieur Martin every time he turns round expecting to see Gerard recounting the old tales of the Camargue and finds a bean pole instead. Nonetheless, without even trying, a miracle of sorts has occurred this afternoon. When the parents of the little children of Cabannes arrive to collect their offspring towards the hour of the aperitif, they find their progenies politely and neatly lined up on their spotted steeds waiting to meet and greet them. And to share the plan of their new teacher, Myrtle Meades:

'Maman, papa – a gymkhana!'

And all the delighted parents nod sagely and with pleasure at Monsieur Martin, Myrtle Meades, the ponies, the children and each other. And as with recent conversations on the other side of the fence that divides the land where an old diseased pear orchard once stood, very few of those present in the paddock have the slightest idea what anyone is talking about. Further, half of the folk in this happy party had no knowledge of, or concern for, clocks that cast warning shadows over them. However, it's of no consequence: those that knew of ticking timepieces have discarded them just as the faint strains of Bulgarian jazz wend their musical way into the almost-here evening. At Phyllida's place, despite the current kitchen carnage, the glasses clink pleasantly. Under a remaining pear tree the ears of a wolf-dog are raised and Clovis whines.

Part Two

Chapter Seven

Jack Shaker and Buddy are in the Bar-Tabac des Alpilles with a few of their pals. They have commandeered a large table at the front of the bar: other ex-pat gentlemen, passing by on their way to purchase yesterday's newspaper, will be able to see them from the tree-lined street that curves around St Remy. There's plenty of room for expected late-comers and the just-plain-nosey. Word has woven its merry way along the ex-pat grapevine. It's a word that has bounced up and down, run back and forth and been well caught at most of the places wherein reside men who speak English as their first language. These are men who erect satellite dishes so they can watch international sports. Men who twist and turn the settings of receptive appliances in order to obtain certain radio commentaries. Men who are heartily sick of pretending to enjoy boules in their gardens. In other words, men who want to play cricket. And some Americans.

Richard 'the giant' Meades has come over from Noves. Along the way, he collected Charlie O'Connor and Nigel Fairbrother. The detritus of their early start to the day now litters the table: leftover cheesy chips, empty coffee cups and half full wine glasses. Underneath the table, Buddy has remained in close proximity to their six legs, in between which many tasty treats have been snatched on their way to the floor of the Bar-Tabac. Also gathered are Lenny Murray and Phil Williams, Dickie Sparrow from Mausanne and Harry Larwood who's made the trip in from Rognonas.

Conversation, if that's what you'd like to call it, has been enthusiastic to say the least. The various discussions, however, have lacked a sense of direction. Jack Shaker, self-appointed group leader, but not-yet-captain, has decided to allow every man his verbal innings before setting an agenda. Monsieur le patron does not possess the psychological insight of Jack Shaker. All Monsieur le patron can see and hear is a bunch of noisy ex-pats shouting and vying for attention.

'Alors, rien ne change', he thinks.

Jack Shaker eventually calls the team to order and announces his intention of making a list. Business is business and without a list it's just not cricket. At the top of a piece of paper, he writes the word 'venue'.

'What we need', says not-yet-Captain Jack, 'are two venues: one to hold the match and another ground on which to practise. Obviously, the location of the practice pitch will be top secret'.

'Why can't the venue for the match be a secret too?' demands Charlie O'Connor.

'Because their side won't turn up', suggests Lenny.

'Easy win for us then', reasons Charlie.

In the same way that the nucleus of the French team has already discovered, identifying a suitable venue for a cricket match in this part of Provence is currently beyond the imagination of any of those presently gathered around the large table at the front of the Bar-Tabac. Given the intense heat of the summer months and the destructive qualities of the mistral, the countryside around the golden triangle is surprisingly lush and verdant. However, given that same superb sunshine and the terrible earth-moving mistral, large areas of grass are particularly thin on the ground. In all senses.

The men make an important decision. They will order one more round of pre-lunch refreshment. Monsieur le patron, having sensed collective confusion, frustration, agitation and thirst, has anticipated another aperitif and is waiting patiently at the head of the table.

'Henri'. It's Richard 'the giant' Meades who dares to speak so informally to Monsieur le patron. Inwardly, Monsieur le patron winces. Outwardly, he retains an air of bonhomie. After all, Richard 'the giant' Meades is one of only a few of these fellows who makes an effort to speak with him in French.

'Henri, have you given any thought to a venue for this cricket match', the giant continues pleasantly?

'Mais oui'. Monsieur le patron elaborates briefly, but politely, before turning towards the bar to fetch the drinks. Turning, one might suggest, wearing the faintest of smiles.

'What did he say', the fledgling team demands?

'Well', replies the giant somewhat despondently, 'it seems their lot have already decided on two locations and it's just a case of them choosing the best for the match'.

'Bloody hell', says Jack Shaker, 'they're well ahead of the game. Didn't realise they were that keen on cricket'.

Monsieur le patron sends his barman, Philippe, over with the replacement drinks and goes outside to make a phone call.

'Christophe? Oui, ça va? The ex-pats are in the bar discussing the cricket. Arguing all morning. Voila, this will be easy. They don't even know where the match will be held mon ami'.

On the other end of the telephone, there is silence. Christophe feels that he's missed something of vital importance.

'Remind me again where it will be?', he asks tentatively.

'Putain! Who knows', comes the shout from St Remy. 'We're not telling them though'.

Chapter Eight

One Saturday morning, early in December, Madame Martin hosts a meeting in her kitchen. During the last three or four weeks, some things that commenced the previous month in the local area have progressed as well as could be expected. These include Phyllida's kitchen renovations, Monsieur Martin's liaison with his new partner and an increase in the cricket-based knowledge possessed in certain sections of the wider community. Alternatively, other matters have not advanced quite as satisfactorily; might have gone downhill, actually. These include the state of Madame Martin's kitchen and her relationship with Madame Lapin.

The meeting that the diminutive lady has called is more by way of an interview with her business partner. Having undertaken a little staff management research sur l'internet, Madame Martin's intention is to attempt some kind of appraisal. Set a few objectives in terms of business loyalty. Reinforce the concept of responsibility. Establish some targets. That sort of thing. It's not going well. Currently, Madame Lapin's head is in mascara-running repose on the table. She is weeping like a demented banshee. Madame Martin had barely begun her plan for time and task supervision when this emotional outburst commenced. Madame Martin is now trying to visualise the staff management website but can't remember reading anything that mentioned thumping fists, hair-pulling or general wailing. She wonders whether Madame Lapin has also been on l'internet: looking up melodrama. For once in her life, Madame Martin is hoping there might be a life-changing knock at the door.

There's a knock at the door. Merde.

Phyllida and Louise have journeyed down the lane to pay a social call on Madame Martin. Phyllida is armed with a home-made vegetable lasagne and, being a self-appointed expert in interior design, a few suggestions regarding the kitchen chez Martin. Louise, being the instigator of all this trouble à la cuisine, is merely present to offer a spot of Dutch courage and support. As far as anyone is aware, the owner of Mas Saint Antoine has not brought anything else along with her. No-one has yet noticed that Nanette, Louise's lady dog, once more in an interesting condition, has silently followed her mistress along the road and down the lane where she is now hiding behind Myrtle Meades' car.

On entering the domain of aborted interviews, the smiles on the faces of Phyllida and Louise soon disappear. Madame Lapin raises a tear-soaked face and sobs a half-hearted, broken-hearted 'bonjour'. The two visitors, one stopping only to place a vegetable lasagne in Madame Martin's tiny hands, rush to the aid of the distraught librarian.

'What's happened?' demands Phyllida.

'Search me', replies Madame Martin. 'She can't speak'.

Louise tries to console the business partner: 'Madame Lapin, are you ill? Has someone died? Has the mediathèque closed down?' Madame Lapin finally pulls herself together and surveys her audience. The audience, sensing imminent news of catastrophic proportions, holds its collective breath.

'It's Jean-Pierre. He's found a younger woman'.

The collective breath of the audience is jointly released. Two of the faces in the audience do their very best to retain an air of concern. The mouth of the third face moves in a somewhat disparaging manner: 'Putain, is that it?' Madame Martin turns to one of her overcrowded shelves and, surprisingly, given the size of her miniscule hands, deftly grabs a bottle and three glasses.

....

Outside, in a corner of the paddock, another member of the household chez Martin also receives a visitor some time hence. There are no vegetable lasagnes in evidence but the occasion is far happier than that currently taking place in the house. Clovis and Nanette have finally found each other again and are celebrating their reunion rather vigorously. In fact, hidden though they are by an overgrowth of paddock-lining brambles, the joyful noises and chaotic disturbance of foliage eventually alerts the attention of Monsieur Martin. With Myrtle Meades in hot pursuit, he dashes to the epicentre of the storm.

'Putain!' Monsieur Martin has spent a life-time dealing with animals but as he dives into the romantic fray, Clovis pauses about his business to offer a particularly unpleasant snarl. One that is reminiscent of the cage-entrapped bad old days. Monsieur Martin takes a step back. 'Fetch Christophe and a stick', he orders Myrtle Meades. And Myrtle bounds to the house and rushes into the kitchen.

The only previous time Myrtle has been in the kitchen chez Martin was when she and Monsieur Martin had first discussed the possibility of working together with the small spotted ponies. Unlike this afternoon's interview in the kitchen-come-office, the earlier business conference had passed reasonably smoothly. Myrtle Meades recalls the interviewer, the interviewer's wife and the interviewee sitting politely around a clean wooden table, each with a small glass of rosé. Conversely, she is rather taken aback at today's gathering. Madame Martin and three other ladies, one of whom seems to be in a particularly bad state of disrepair, are seated around that very same table, likewise with a glass each. There the similarity and any sense of order ends. Reader, if I tell you that an assortment of alcohol infused bottles, variously filled or empty, are also scattered about the kitchen-or-office table, you might be better left to imagining the demeanour of those seated or sprawled. Myrtle Meades, being well-read, is minded of a scene from Chaucer. Possibly, the *Wife of Bath*.

'Is that her?' demands Madame Lapin rather aggressively.

'Who?' the other pilgrims reply.

'Who?' asks Myrtle Meades. Myrtle suddenly remembers why she's unexpectedly burst upon this scene of Provençal decadence. 'I need Christophe', she exclaims.

'I bet you do', leers Madame Lapin.

'And a stick', Myrtle continues.

'Naturally; nothing like a good beating', the wretched librarian sobs.

Myrtle Meades, with a stiff British upper lip, tries her very best to ignore the confusion and carnage. 'It's Clovis. He's captured a small yellow lady dog and now he's attacking Monsieur Martin in the brambles'.

'Merde, my baby', cries Louise as she pushes back her chair, stands up and immediately falls over.

Chapter Nine

Christmas passes almost before anyone has noticed its arrival. However, it would be foolish of your narrator to allow this opportunity for consolidation to wend its merry way into history without comment. Let's face it, Christmas is a time to relax and gently mull over the preceding year's events before commencing anew. Pardon? Madame Martin feels there's little opportunity to relax in her ever-shrinking, increasingly dilapidated kitchen: a kitchen constantly full of all and sundry bringing their emotional baggage à table to which we will return shortly.

At home, any home, one is often expected to pass the season of goodwill with those family members to whom the least amount of goodwill is voluntarily expended during other times of the year. It's a bit different for the ex-pats in Provence who have made a new life in distant climes. For a start, they wouldn't have moved to the South if they had any desire to be in regular contact with many of their biological relatives. They certainly wouldn't have chosen to live along the road that runs between Noves and Cabannes if they wanted to be easily found. But, for most of them, there's an ingrained debt to this cultural business of sharing seasonal bonhomie. It's true that the partner who cannot be named has little interest in stories linked to stars and stables. Neither has he much of an appetite for the giving of expensive gifts, or cheap ones. The partner has been a little grumpy of late owing to the onset of a tediously dull pain in his lower back. Phyllida has taken him to Noves where Dr Giraud was unable to determine the reason; largely because wooden chaise longues were absent from any account of possible causal activities. He has advised a course of yoga. Phyllida is extremely happy with this prescription as the partner will now be able to accompany her to the centre culturel once a week. The partner is less than happy.

In the meantime, they have shared a festive dinner with Louise, Louise's visiting (and possibly welcome) mother and Louise's lawn-mowing husband. Myrtle and Richard Meades were also in attendance. The appearance of these extra guests was also a source of dismay to the partner who cannot be named as, in his opinion, far too much conversation was exhausted on the subject of cricket. Nonetheless, there may have been a geographical resolution of sorts. Louise's husband has offered to mow a wicket in their parkland in order that the ex-pat team has a practice venue. Apart from the minor irritation of the sports interlude, which was easily managed with a few extra aperitifs, the celebrations were enjoyable.

Louise, as everyone agrees, is an excellent chef. She has managed to secure a large goose on the table whilst simultaneously producing a succulent nut roast for her vegetarian neighbours. To aid her culinary expertise, she has, of course, the advantage of owning the best available in the departments of kitchen equipment and utensils. The Norwegian Blues, meanwhile, have been left at home with platefuls of gourmet goodies fit for their delicate palates. Nanette, however, being the pampered lady of Mas Saint Antoine when guest dogs are absent, is resplendent in her self-contained exhibitionism. She lies on her back in front of the fire, legs stuck at various angles, displaying a rather distended tummy. She looks full of goose. Louise tries hard not to look at Nanette. Louise knows only too well that it's not a goose which lurks inside her beloved lady dog. Like the spring flowers that currently lie dormant beneath the gardens of Provence, the thing that is not a goose waits to make an appearance. Unlike the golden crocuses, the not-a-goose-in-waiting has more to do with a wolf dog than floral adornments that might have been planted for the delight of early-in-the-year holiday makers.

Over at chez Martin, the celebrations have also been in full swing but were not undertaken with the advantages of an avant garde kitchen. The last thing that Madame Martin thinks about is the potential paternal responsibilities of Clovis. Of these, she has no idea as she batters her tiny route around the kitchen of despair. Was it so long ago, she wonders, that she accompanied Monsieur Villiers to see the santons in the crèche at Frigolet? How she would have loved to see the seasonal display in the town hall of Tarasçon. Poor Tarasçon: vilified throughout the year for its nerve to sit adjacent to smelly Beaucaire, suddenly redeems itself each Christmastide with the most extraordinary account of Provençal social history. The miniscule clay visitors wend their supplicating way up the stairs of the Hôtel de Ville, round the corner to the epicentre of the nativity and yet again celebrate the arrival of Jesus in Provence.

Madame Lapin has been celebrating the arrival of, amongst others, Jean-Pierre Lucard. In this, she has imbibed more than one aperitif as she considers that, had Daudet been alive and present chez elle this Christmastide, he almost certainly would have felt obliged to write a prominent paella purveyor into correspondence from his windmill. There are, of course, others: Christophe, Netty and her father who has travelled from the Camargue, Monsieur Martin, Sophie, Dr Giraud and the obligatory goose. Nut roasts, however, do not comprise an element of this gathering. Nut roasts comprise an unknown concept at the bottom of the lane that runs from the road between Noves and Cabannes.

Since the errant Jean-Pierre Lucard returned to the fold, Madame Lapin is a changed woman from the one who attended that distressing interview earlier in the month. Mascara, for example, now accentuates a pair of bright eyes rather than running in lava-like rivulets down red, puffy cheeks. Hair has been piled high with deliberately falling wisps shaping that not-really-enigmatic face. Of course, clothing has been chosen with care: the right parts of the body are emphasised and the not-so-good quarters are pleasantly disguised. And everything has been dressed with a variety of sparkling and seasonal adornments: earrings, necklaces and a bracelet that proudly sits below Madame Lapin's sleeve, next to the place where she wears her heart.

Jean-Pierre Lucard is still wearing his summer ensemble. Come hell or high wind, both of which have made more than one appearance during the preceding autumn, the paella purveyor, immune to meteorological inconsistencies, can be depended upon in the department of sartorial. The pale pink shirt is currently replaced by one in a pleasant shade of grey. Naturally, in the winter warmth of the kitchen chez Martin, he's been able to open a few buttons and his golden medallion shines like a gift from a passing king. Actually, in this part of the world, the kings don't pass this way until epiphany, at which point vast amounts of gateaux will be eaten; and numerous admissions to the Henri Duffaut hospital in Avignon will witness mass choking on miniature cartoon characters hidden in the depths of the epiphany cakes. In the meantime, Jean-Pierre Lucard also sports a glinting wrist. The person who once dared to call herself a feminist has given her lover an identity bracelet with her own name engraved upon.

Amongst other gifts, Madame Lapin has donated an enormous bunch of mistletoe which now hangs on a handy nail above the kitchen table. Each time someone stands up, they are knocked sideways by the foliage and berries fall like poisonous snowflakes into the food below. 'Putain', thinks Madame Martin although, secretly, she's delighted to have her friend and business partner back on board. What's really annoying her, however, is the continuous talk of cricket. How times change. Let's be clear, this is Provence. People flock to Provence precisely because things don't change. Generally. When was the last time someone suggested holding a cricket match in a bull-ring?

From the clear winter skies above chez Martin, the faintest of passing sleigh bells might be heard by anyone who is not busy celebrating. And in his secret grotto under the festive table Clovis lifts a quizzical ear and whines.

Chapter Ten

It's a funny old time, New Year's Eve. Those in the golden circle who are wrapped in a blanket of ex-pat security are generally the ones who host the grand cosmopolitan parties attended by a variety of guests. All have reinvented themselves in the unknowing and largely uncaring South and have invited one or two unsuspecting French neighbours to give the occasion (and accompanying photos) a sense of authenticity. Amidst the deepness of mid-winter that permeates the South, flurries of coldness still retain their prerogative to fall unrequested on ground reserved for sunflowers, irises, and all things Provençal. And, despite having witnessed this before, everyone rushes outside to touch the snow as if it was a previously unseen meteorological phenomenon. Paradoxically, although they've moved to Provence precisely to avoid this type of inconvenient weather, they are warmed by its appearance. They are reminded of home and their parties are comprised of knowledgeable guests relishing the opportunity to recount historical difficulties in traversing the slippery paths of England and her colonies. In this, they hold the centre, but icy, ground; being superior in experience to the French but still below par when it comes to guests from New York, New York. Yes, we heard you the first time.

Most of us, regardless of where we reside, despise the illusion of bonhomie which fails to thwart our suspicions that this year more of that which passed in previous years will prevail. On the other and more optimistic hand, there are some folk who feel that small deviations will lead to greater changes. Madame Lapin, for example, has shunned an invitation to see in yet another year at the bottom of the lane that runs from the road between Noves and Cabannes. Always the party-goer, Madame Lapin has had a better offer. Well, in truth, it was our latter day feminist who made the suggestion of dinner for two in her bijou apartment in Cabannes. The recipient of this kindly invitation is currently resplendent in the golden chain that adorns his strong neck, the brand new silver identity bracelet that hangs around his chunky wrist and little else apart from his also dangling manhood. Madame Lapin, in her own private manger, is enjoying the arrival of her epiphany king.

The table is strewn with the detritus of réveillon: a plate of tell-tale oyster shells goes some way to explaining a selection of hastily discarded garments that covers the floor of the bijou apartment. Dishes of roast lamb and succulent winter vegetables remain abandoned at the scene of dinner – those mischievous molluscs having weaved their aphrodisiacal spell over the proceedings at une bonne heure. The second course subsequently comprised a great deal more interaction than could ever be imagined with a dead sheep. To be fair, Madame Lapin was rather looking forward to the lamb which she had cooked oh-so-slowly with all the anticipation reserved for an intimate meal devoid of paella. Par contre, Jean-Pierre Lucard was a little dismayed to see no early sign of his favourite dish and, having satisfied one type of hunger via the shellfish, had moved hastily on to dealing with another appetite.

It starts with a foot. A foot devoid of woolly winter socks. A foot which, in the dark recesses under the dinner table, begins a journey upwards from an ankle it has discovered. The owner of the ankle has recently resumed her seat which was temporarily vacated in order to fetch more of the wine that fills the diners with the warmth of the Rhône Valley. The ankle bears a bracelet fit for an Egyptian queen. The naked foot has not previously noticed this adornment and there is a momentary hitch in affairs as an unwieldy toenail becomes entangled with a delicate and supposedly seductive chain. 'Merde', splutters the naked foot. 'What's this nonsense?' as it pulls away from the unwanted (at this stage) bondage. In so doing, the delicate and supposedly seductive chain snaps. 'Putain', retorts the now unadorned ankle. The foot and the ankle put on respective brave faces and the one begins a second ascent of the other. Meanwhile, above the table, Madame Lapin and Jean-Pierre Lucard each take another large swig of the red stuff in preparation for the business ahead.

They look knowingly into each other's eyes although, as the naked foot arrives at the summit of a kneecap, the eyes of Madame Lapin begin to disappear into an unseen chasm somewhere above her recently threaded eyebrows. Also unseen, are curling toes underneath the table that do not belong to the intrepid exploring foot. Jean-Pierre, greatly encouraged by this apparent swooning and a noticeable change in breathing patterns, croons to the heart that belongs to the knee, ankle and curly toes: 'chérie, chérie'. And egged on by the now completely hidden eyes, the rapid breathing technique and the beating of the crooned heart, the foot below the shell encrusted table expertly moves in search of a thigh or two.

Considering this is a bijou apartment, Madame Lapin has been surprisingly adept in her introduction of a reasonably sized table. A table is, after all, très important: not only does it have to be big enough to warrant the invitation of others to eat, it does, on less auspicious occasions, serve other purposes. For example, Madame Lapin uses hers to read on, to deal with her business documentation, to discuss the ever expanding jam and pickle website via her laptop, to rebuild her early morning face with a hated but essential magnifying mirror and so forth. Yes, there's no doubt that a table of a reasonable size is central to the maintenance of a well-ordered lifestyle. Not so good though if you want to reach a pair of thighs opposite a roaming foot whilst retaining a casual but upright position.

That naughty, naked foot, having almost completed a successful assault on one thigh, excitedly lunges for its final destination. However, even an infant could see that there's a mathematical improbability involved regarding the size of the foot, the length of the adjoining leg and the distance between Jean-Pierre's seat and his ultimate goal. The paella purveyor discovers this mathematical conundrum too late in the day. Enticed by a crescendo of moaning from the other side of the reasonably sized table, Jean-Pierre Lucard totally misjudges feet, inches and metres as he slides off his chair into the darkness below.

As the eyes of Madame Lapin reside somewhere in the back of her skull at this point, she fails to see the disappearance of her lover and thinks the arrival of his head between her thighs to be a promising turn of events. At another time, on another day, Jean-Pierre might agree. Now, however, he finds himself somewhat compromised by the bulk of his macho body and the lack of space beneath the tablecloth, amongst the many wooden and human legs. Further, the most masculine element of Jean-Pierre's usually macho body is no longer either macho or bulky. The heart and brain of Madame Lapin send confusing signs to each other during which they recommend the eyes of the librarian to return to their usual resting place and reopen themselves. The brain, heart and newly functioning eyes of this good lady then send warning signals to the knees below the table which immediately respond by clamping themselves together. Well, as together as they can manage with Jean-Pierre's head in between.

It's little wonder that these two finally adjourn to the bedroom. What's more surprising is that either of them retains any interest in the continuation of the main course. Madame Lapin, for example, is mourning the loss of her new ankle bracelet and her cherished shoulder of epiphany lamb. And, like most women, the sudden cessation of foreplay, or in this case footplay, has not been conducive to an immediate resumption of activities. It's different for men. Once he's extricated himself from the depths of geographical and amorous demise beneath the table, Jean-Pierre is more than ready to get going once more in his desire to welcome in the New Year with a bang. And like most men, having already indulged in one spot of seasonal foreplay, he sees no reason to start again from scratch.

Jean-Pierre Lucard embarks his hostess and sets sail on the good ship Lapin. Stormy seas cause an excess of swaying and the erstwhile feminist is clipped about the masthead a couple of times by the gold and silver links of her lover's armoury. Jean-Pierre, rides out his imaginary storm like a salty old sea-dog and 'land ahoy' is finally called while Madame Lapin is still quietly contemplating the little sheep in a pot à table.

Part Three

Chapter Eleven

January is cold and nature is best left to its own devices. The earth in the gardens on Phyllida's side of the fence is too hard for current cultivation and the partner who cannot be named has finally been forced to return to the kitchen. There's no longer any escape from the tiling and grouting: walls and floor must be attended to in order that sumptuous new recipes can be experimented with in preparation for entertaining in the warmer months. Entertaining that can only proceed once Phyllida has erected and installed new shelves to house bottles and jars, and tins and pans, and openers and closers, and all varieties of kitchen implements. Phyllida is going for the rustic look. In truth, Phyllida's kitchen previously epitomised the rustic look but this was deemed too authentic. The type of rusticity now in vogue is more modern, in a retro kind of way. And speaking of bottles and jars, the style currently under review in a kitchen on the other side of the fence has not yet achieved rusticity in any of its incarnations, being still more medieval in nature. So, whilst the partner is busily occupied in one kitchen, Phyllida and Louise have journeyed down the lane that runs from the road between Noves and Cabannes in a car that drags a trailer behind it.

This mode of transport might seem a little excessive given the short distance. However, in the trailer is a selection of cast-offs from the kitchens of Phyllida and Louise. Madame Martin has no problem with taking these off the hands of her neighbours. She likes the way the ex-pats don't think twice about sharing. Spending money on kitchens has never been top of a list of priorities that Monsieur Martin might have written. In fact, spending money on kitchens has never featured at any stage of a list that Monsieur Martin might have constructed had he ever made a list of priorities. For this reason, Monsieur Martin is not immediately in evidence. At least the partner who cannot be named knows that he must occasionally donate a few hours of his time to renovations. This concept is unlikely to ever bear credence with Monsieur Martin and the new fixtures and fittings in his house will be fixed and fitted without his direct assistance.

Over two or three days, the women naturally make a good job of things. On the third day, Myrtle Meades calls by chez Martin to offer help with the small spotted ponies. Sadly, given the hard, frost-bitten ground, there's little to do once fresh straw has been distributed. Monsieur Martin, having made a statement of sorts regarding all things kitchen-related, is, nonetheless, currently engaged on work of the utmost importance. His task has nothing to do with ponies, peppers and pears as they appear in the more prosaic parts of his life. It does, however, play a potentially major part in the world-wide spread of confiture and the increasingly global demand for Provençal pickle. Monsieur Martin is laying the literal foundations of a business extension that will house an office for the two bonnes madames. One of these madames has recently decided that the enterprise might regain a notion of greater economic efficiency if the other madame is geographically located, at least during the working day, in closer proximity to the hub of pickle production. Madame Martin is not keen on this 'working from home' phenomenon. She considers that the potential for distraction in Madame Lapin's bijou apartment is too – well, distracting.

A brand new, purpose-built bureau des affaires might be just the thing to encourage Madame Lapin back into the corporate enclave. Of course, whilst the office will be new in one sense – that being the sense of having one's stilettoed feet firmly on different ground – it's not entirely true to call the structure purpose-built. Once the shiny new cement floor has been created and has dried, Monsieur Martin, with the help of favour-owing friends, will move a redundant hen-house into its new position outside the kitchen and onto the office floor.

Myrtle Meades, having accomplished all she can for the ponies this morning, is at a bit of a loose end. Now, she also finds herself redundant in the cement making and spreading departments which, not to put too finer point on it, is deemed men's work in this part of the world. She has taken a sneaky and wistful look through the kitchen window and is wishing she could be a useful part of activities indoors. Thus, it happens that, whilst hanging around wondering what to do with herself, her attention is assaulted by the sounds of shrieking emanating from within. Myrtle looks to Monsieur Martin for confirmation that help might be required by the international kitchen renovators. Monsieur Martin is busy with a shovel and an ancient cement mixer that he's borrowed from somewhere or other. He's sporting a pair of ear protectors that he's also purloined from some unknown source. Although the cement mixer is mixing cement in a rather half-hearted, vaguely-murmuring way, there's no suggestion that the ear protectors are either working or even necessary. Neither is there any indication of whether shrieks can even be heard, let alone whether they might be responded to.

Myrtle Meades decides, with some reticence, that it's her duty to investigate whether she can help in the kitchen. The last time she visited the domain of Madame Martin the place was nothing short of carnage. On that occasion, it was, as it is now, also inhabited by Phyllida and Louise. However, Madame Martin's business partner, who had taken such a terrible dislike to Myrtle at that time, is, today, conspicuous by her absence. In those split seconds that lose any temporal sense and evolve into a period long enough for analytical recall, Myrtle also remembers that on the same sorry day that Clovis had cornered both Nanette and Monsieur Martin in the bramble bushes, the room that she's just appeared in had been unable to make up its mind whether it was, in fact, a kitchen, a bar or an office; its owners having overwhelmed it with conflicting demands. Today, it's clear that this area of chez Martin is determined to claim sole identity as a cuisine and is busily trying to embrace the new shelves and cupboards that the ladies from the other side of various fences have delivered.

Despite being a large and practical woman, Myrtle Meades experiences just a suggestion of anxiety about her presence in the place where she was so previously vilified. However, it's evident that the kitchen renovators, despite having already accomplished so much, are currently struggling under the pressure of a particularly unwieldy piece of Swedish kitchenalia. In truth, not only are they under pressure, but one of them, Phyllida to be precise, has somehow become trapped under whatever the Swedish steel item might turn out to be.

Myrtle Meades leaps into action. Hardly gazelle-like, this is no time for aesthetics and she quickly releases Phyllida from the confines of a soon-to-be potential pickle pan store. The cosmopolitan kitchen renovators are extremely grateful. Louise guides the Swedish monstrosity into the centre of the kitchen where, latterly, the old wooden table used for eating, chopping and occasional interviews once stood.

Madame Martin is confused: 'what are you doing?' she asks Louise.

'It's an island unit', explains Louise. Myrtle and the recently liberated Phyllida can see that this elucidation has done nothing to dispel Madame Martin's confusion.

'An island?' It's difficult to say whether it's the word that's been lost in translation, its context within this particular kitchen, the concept of something possibly intended to resemble a miniature version of Sardinia at the bottom of the lane that runs from the road between Noves and Cabannes, or none of the above. Phyllida, attempting clarification, has never had the opportunity to introduce an island unit into her own kitchen. This is not to say that she has never dreamed of wandering round such an island, cutting and chopping, slicing and beating, whisking and folding whilst talking knowledgably with a crowd of admiring onlookers who are beside themselves with pride at having been invited to eat at such a venerable residence.

Sadly, Phyllida has never owned a kitchen of sufficient size to accommodate an island unit. Further, it's most unlikely that any of Phyllida's guests on the other side of the fence would ever step inside to stand and stare while she performed for their delight. Phyllida's guests are the type of people who enjoy sitting in her wonderful garden as the sun goes down, clutching a large glass of something refreshing. These folk prefer to look outwards at the few remaining pear trees whose branches rays of the aged sun defiantly penetrate. Phyllida's guests are delighting in the decreasing whir of the cicadas whilst looking forward to the singing frogs and the first familiar call of the evening owls. They are content to have their glass replenished whilst quietly nibbling on one or two of the juiciest black olives that Provence can provide. Not for them the uncomfortable (and let's be fair, tedious) voyeurism involved in watching someone else prepare dinner.

'Might be different if you were watching a world class chutney chef', suggests Phyllida optimistically at the close of her almost-Shakespearean soliloquy to persuade Madame Martin of the advantages of a well-placed island unit.

'Putain', explodes Madame Martin. 'It's a working kitchen in Provence, not bloody Mont Saint Michel'. Translated, this means that the kitchen table is at the heart of the house and thus lives at the centre of the kitchen. Louise and Phyllida are momentarily shocked at this unexpected outburst and look crestfallen. Myrtle Meades, as one who might once have been trained as a foreign diplomat, quickly takes stock of the situation. Before the Swedish steel island can become the centre of dispute in international waters, she pushes it into a space alongside one wall where it finally finds a home as part of the Provençal coastal shelf of this particular kitchen.

Madame Martin looks round guiltily at the friendly kitchen renovators. 'I'm sorry', she begins, 'it's just that ...'

Louise interrupts her: 'Madame Martin, it's *your* new kitchen and *you* must choose where everything goes.' Madame Martin smiles gratefully at her cosmopolitan companions. 'If we could just bring the table back in, we could have a little drink to toast the new kitchen'.

No sooner said than done. The four women retrieve the kitchen table from its temporary resting place outside the front door and return it to the location of its greatest service and well-being in the centre of the kitchen. The table heaves a sigh of relief and the ladies fill their glasses which they raise to each other and to the results of their hard work. In that first warm taste of liquid Provence, Myrtle Meades relishes not only an especial sense of calm, but also the perception of belonging; she finally feels part of something important.

Louise takes centre stage as she addresses Madame Martin: 'there's something I need to give you'.

'Mais, non, non,' their hostess interrupts. 'You've already given so much. What else can I possibly need?'

'Puppies', replies her neighbour.

Ensconced under the newly replaced table, Clovis whines.

Chapter Twelve

Something unusual is going on over at Mas Saint Antoine. Monsieur Martin, despite the replacement of a table in the centre of the kitchen, is sick to his small rear molars of all the recent disruption chez Martin. In particular, he's extremely fed up with constant observations concerning the obvious distance between the new office floor and the old hen house. Madame Martin is like a stuck record: 'When will the Bureau des Affaires be ready?' from dusk till dawn. 'How's a global enterprise supposed to function without an office?'

Even the business partner has started joining in the collective nagging: 'Bonjour Monsieur Martin. Any movement on the office front?' asks Madame Lapin every time she spots the weary husband. These women don't seem to understand how difficult it is to get the men together with the small crane that's necessary to lift up the hen house and replace it on the new floor. Everyone's busy: things to do, people to see, crops to plant and so on. Monsieur Martin and Clovis just want a bit of peace and quiet. They have, accordingly, taken themselves for a walk, way past Phyllida's place, to the far end of what remains of the old pear orchard. Clovis, always keen on a stroll in company, is particularly happy to be stepping out in this direction. They're following one of his old tracks to the place where his chérie resides and Clovis is pretty sure there's extra canine activity afoot. But, as the two approach the boundary of Mas Saint Antoine, they become aware that something unexpected is occurring. Something that involves more boundaries of one sort or another.

The shouts of men first alert the two ramblers. Mas Saint Antoine, at least during the warmer months, is advertised as an up-market haven of rural calm away from the noise of Avignon and the market-driven hustle and bustle of St Remy. Today, however, it sounds like a city-centre building site. Well, what Monsieur Martin imagines an English city-centre building site might sound like as none of the voices are French. However, before they can investigate further, their attention is drawn to a rather curious scene. Alongside the perimeter fence, at a point where the golden showering blossom of a newly flowering mimosa bush offers cover from the sight of those looking out, but visual access for those looking in, sits a man. This stealthy observer has a shock of white hair that seems to reflect both age and wisdom. The wise old voyeur is busy writing at speed in a moleskin notebook. It's a particularly admirable feat as the wise, white-haired writer is sitting in a very upright position, legs crossed, with each sandaled foot resting on its opposite thigh. The partner who cannot be named, following a few torturous sessions of yoga at the community centre, has assumed the lotus position.

'Bonjour, mon ami', Monsieur Martin greets his neighbour. Keeping your back straight, your legs crossed, your feet fixed on their opposite thighs at the same time as covertly observing the action through a fence and writing in a moleskin notebook is fairly demanding. The partner who cannot be named has been concentrating hard on simultaneously managing such a variety of challenges and he has no idea that anyone else is in the vicinity. When Monsieur Martin speaks, the partner is so surprised that, in turning in the direction of the greeting, he topples sideways in what can only be described as an unfortunate knot. Clovis rushes over and licks the partner's face in a friendly and enthusiastic attempt to make things better. The partner who cannot be named does not seem particularly impressed with the wolf-dog's slavering kindness but Monsieur Martin arrives to untangle his neighbour and help him to his feet before Clovis can become the butt of unwarranted abuse. It seems that the partner, however, is not keen on standing.

'Get down, get down', he hisses at Monsieur Martin. 'I don't want that lot to know I'm here'. Monsieur Martin looks through the golden mimosa blooms and over the perimeter fence in the direction that his neighbour is nodding.

In Provence, when driving along a road in the early months of the year, it's possible, or even probable, for the unknowing traveller to find themselves accosted by an unexpected sense of sunlit intrusion. You pull over suddenly to the side of the road and undertake further inspection. It's difficult to comprehend. In essence, it's still winter, yet here is everything that seems to epitomise the colours of Provence before they're due. It's the mimosa. Monsieur Martin, having been lucky enough to have lived in the South for more years than this story intends to reveal, is not as startled by yellow as others. He is, however, somewhat astonished as he beholds the second curious sight of the morning. Although the ground is still hard, there are a number of men situated at various points around what will, at some later point in the year, comprise a lawn. One or two of them seem to be running between a couple of wooden struts.

'What's going on here?' he asks his neighbour. 'Cricket', the note-taker responds.

Time to take a step away from perimeters and boundaries and suchlike. Time to go back in time to a point where Jack Shaker has tried to get a team together. It's not a French thing: in this busy world, people of all nationalities are reticent to commit to anything. Especially retired people. There's too much else to do. Too many places to be seen in. For example, it's vital to be seen eating cassoulet in Le Paradou in the winter months. It's necessary to be organising one's spare rooms for occupation in the summer. And so on and so forth. But somehow, Jack Shaker has managed to persuade most of the ex-pats that participation in the who-knows-when cricket match is de rigueur, even if they don't know that that means.

Accordingly, Harry Larwood, Richard Meades, Charlie O'Connor and several others are currently engaged in their first practice of the season. Of course, the real match, whenever, if ever, will involve France v Rest of the World. Today's game, however, is more in the region of one team against whoever is batting at any given time. It's a good opportunity for Captain Jack to assess the skills of various players. In this, he is helped by Dickie Sparrow who is currently the self-appointed umpire. It's not really the weather for cricket whites so Dickie is clothed in his own winter coat plus the scarves and hats of batsmen Nigel Fairbrother and Lenny Murray who have somehow managed to rack up fourteen runs between them.

Monsieur Martin is fascinated by the action on the other side of the fence. The partner who cannot be named has regained a position of measured breathing and is trying, in whispered tones, to explain some of the finer points of cricket that he has garnered from reading the website of The Museum of English Rural Life and from watching this morning's activities. Of particular interest to the partner is the discovery that many of the forty two laws of cricket are concerned with the amount of time played as determined by the intake of refreshment.

'For example', he explains confidently, 'the laws relate to what has happened before and after lunch and before and after tea'.

'What about coffee?' asks Monsieur Martin. The partner is, like the ball on the other side of the fence, momentarily thrown.

'No ball', shouts Dickie Sparrow.

'No coffee', states the partner.

Although Monsieur Martin is taken aback at the news of the absence of coffee, he is more surprised by Dickie Sparrow's call which, although in English, is easily translated. 'What does he mean 'no ball'? The ball is still there', he says.

'Well', says the expert under the mimosa, 'you can have no ball or short ball'.

'How many balls are there altogether?' asks Monsieur Martin in some confusion as he looks for evidence of the others.

'Oh, just the one', replies the partner. But before Monsieur Martin can ask for clarification, another call is heard from the Mas Saint Antoine ground:

'Lost ball'. And this is followed by more shouting that would be difficult to understand by the most bi-lingual of expert cricket commentators as, despite it being neither lunch nor tea-time, the match is abandoned in noisy confusion. Angry players try to corner a wolf-dog who now holds the one and only ball in his greasy jaws. For while the two interested parties under the mimosa have been busy trying to comprehend some of the forty two laws, the disregarded Clovis has spotted an opportunity to shimmy under a known-only-to-him weakness in the fence.

Clovis has no interest whatsoever in cricket. He knows that Nanette is somewhere out of sight on the Mas Saint Antoine estate. Further, he has an irrational notion that his chérie may not be alone. Clovis doesn't understand his own doggy confusion that is driving him forward. Unlike Jean-Pierre Lucard, Clovis feels there might be more than canine or carnal fulfilment to seek out. Clovis is a dog so it doesn't occur to him to stop for chocolates or flowers. However, he has an inexplicable feeling that a gift might be in order so, on his way across the parkland pitch, he collects a handy red leather ball that's rolling around. Louise, who also has about as much knowledge of the forty two rules as Monsieur Martin's dog, has chosen this moment to emerge from the house in her role as dutiful hostess with a tray of Madelines and tiny designer styled cups of steaming black coffee. Coffee and Madelines fly across the patio as Clovis, ball clamped firmly between his jaws, runs between her legs and locates his darling Nanette in the kitchen. Clovis, like many a male before him, drops the cricket ball as he screeches to a halt in front of his unknown and unexpected new family.

'Putain'. This from Clovis. This also from Monsieur Martin and the partner who cannot be named. Neither of these two can see the puppies but they both share a desire to leave this scene as quickly and silently as possible.

'Dead ball', shouts Dickie Sparrow. But no-one is listening.

Chapter Thirteen

Madame Martin is also taking a walk. She begins by slamming a door and striding purposively down the lane. However, on reaching the junction with that infamous road that runs between Noves and Cabannes, she's at a bit of a loss. The initial bad temper, caused by missing dogs and rumours of new mother-like canine responsibilities, errant husbands and non-existent offices, island units and over-helpful neighbours well – life in general, has reached breaking point. But, having successfully bypassed Phyllida's place without being spotted, she's run out of decisive intentions.

Madame Martin doesn't want to turn right because, at this point in time, Cabannes, for a number of reasons, holds no truck for her. On the other hand, she doesn't want to turn left as this will involve passing Mas Saint Antoine which, if rumour is to be believed, seems to be full of amateur cricketers and puppies devoid of fathers. The puppies that is, not the cricketers. Crossing the road is a non-starter as this entails delicately sidestepping winter-full navigation channels only to wander aimlessly into undiseased orchards. Madame Martin weighs up the limited options, resists a passing temptation to return home for coffee and turns left.

For all the infamy attributed to the road that runs between Noves and Cabannes in these and other pages, this minor route is not the epitome of all things Provençal from a tourist's perspective. To be fair, your average visitor wouldn't deviate from their journey along the N7 between Avignon and St Andiol. And to be even fairer, they wouldn't be going from Avignon to St Andiol along the N7 in the first place unless they were lost; or had, by some miracle of serendipity, have heard about the Chemin de la Liberté and the local and national hero, Jean Moulin. No, largely, the road between Noves and Cabannes is famous only in literary tomes for the people that happen to live along the way.

Madame Martin, head down, successfully bypasses Mas Saint Antoine. She feels a little guilty for ignoring her kitchen donating neighbour, the cricketers and the noise that she assumes to be caused by her intrusive dog. She passes the domaine of old Monsieur Regnier and notices, sadly, the dying Plane trees that wither their sorry way along the route to his last home on this earth. Madame Martin has amassed the knowledge and lore of the country from her sometimes irrelevant husband and from the long gone days of television quiz shows. She knows the death of the trees is not another symbol of climate change. Let's face it, it's so hot here most of the time, it would be difficult to recognise another two degrees of sun. Madame Martin, global in other ways and patriotic to the core, believes, correctly, that the death of the Plane trees began years ago when the fungus-ridden foreign boots of so-called allies walked the land. And what's a pickle purveyor supposed to do?

What goes round comes round she ponders philosophically. In summers past, French students, alongside a smattering of those from England or Holland, would have arrived here to collect succulent fruit harvests. Now, older workers from countries whose names are difficult to pronounce reap the sulky harvests. A kind of seasonal diaspora of poorer men without a sense of achievement or wonder at the offerings of the South. There's little knowledge of the fruits of Provence if you fail to traverse this glorious market garden on a regular basis. On one hand, Madame Martin feels sorry for today's foreigners who miss the year of the countryside. On the other, she's pleased to have it to herself this morning. And many other mornings.

Madame Martin trudges on. She crosses the weed-throttled, abandoned single track railway along which a little engine traversed the fields in times past, dragging trucks of apricots and apples, pears and plums. She strolls alongside a canal where, she remembers, coypu once swam. Before the fleeting memory can disappear back into the well of younger years, a flash of black catches her eye and Madame stops to study the water more carefully. Perhaps it was a rat? Two magpies, disturbed by her presence, ascend from the bank to a treetop and the scene reverts to one of silence. Madame Martin turns back to the road but the water is once again disturbed and suddenly she spots the aquatic guinea-pig amongst the reeds. It's an unexpected treat. She hasn't seen the coypu in five years but here, on this winter morning, it quite unexpectedly performs for her solitary benefit. Madame Martin, enlivened, decides to cross the main road and walk into Noves.

Feeling the need to justify her unplanned visit, Madame Martin purchases two baguettes from the boulangerie. Many of the tables outside the scruffy bar in the centre of the village have been commandeered by locals enjoying the mid-morning sunshine. Madame exchanges Bonjours with faces known and unknown but, not feeling sufficiently full of bonhomie for further conversation, finds an empty place to enjoy her coffee. She breaks off a tiny portion from one of the baguettes and eats it slowly in a world where little exists apart from the brief memory of the coypu. However, another memory is about make an unexpected entry into her reverie.

As Madame Martin raises the tiny coffee cup to her lips, a battered old red car passes along the road in front of this Michelin starless place of refreshment. It would have been a moment of indescribable insignificance had the driver had not braked suddenly and reversed at great speed to a point directly in front of Madame's table. All of the heads of all of the al fresco coffee and Pastis drinkers at Bar de la République simultaneously turn in the direction of this welcome disturbance in their lives. All of the eyes in all of the heads, including those of the pickle purveyor, scan the interior of the car in search of the identity of the driver. It's a tricky task. At first, it seems that there is no driver; that somehow, the magic red car has woven its intrusive way through the middle of Noves before making a sudden decision to screech backwards to its current resting place. But our global chutney chef has spotted a mass of black curls beneath the steering wheel of the red car and knows only too well who has espied her on this winter sun-soaked morning:

'Madame Martin, bonjour', exclaims Monsieur Villiers with, it must be said, some joy as he steps from his automated confines.

And our dear Madame, who, up until this moment, thinks that there is nothing left in the world to startle her, other than kitchen islands and the unexpected appearance of an aquatic guinea-pig, is completely wrong-footed.

'Monsieur Villiers', she responds with a large, unseen question mark. A question mark that hovers uncertainly over her whole being. A question mark that invites a tentative, polite embrace that precedes an invitation to sit. And a seating that calls for two glasses of rather early-in-the-day rosé. Two glasses of rosé that terminate any interest on the part of other customers who duly resume their places in the quotidian.

Chapter Fourteen

Reader, you know by now that, having arrived at a particular point in time, your narrator generally moves elsewhere. However, it's been so many months since Monsieur Villiers graced our stories of the South an exception must be made to the norm. I want to know what he's doing here!

Notwithstanding quizzes and parades, cricket and yoga, aperitifs and chutney, the very favourite pursuit of the French is conversation. These people are professional talkers. Politics is a popular topic of course, but two hours on the price of melons is also easily accomplished. There's a lot of time to be accounted for since Madame Martin last met the vet from Plan d'Orgon. And as talking is a national pastime, and because they're on their second glass of rosé, neither of our protagonists feel uncomfortable. In fact, as Monsieur Villiers has already shared his happy memories of their long-ago trip to the abbey at Frigolet, and the extraordinary display of santons, Madame Martin has no qualms about expressing her disappointment at missing the crèche in Tarascon. So, it's the catalyst for an impromptu outing. It's too late for Tarascon, in more than one sense. However, Monsieur Villiers, ever the intrepid explorer, has another suggestion on this sunny (in more than one sense) morning.

'Madame Martin', he begins, 'have you ever been to Barbegal?'

For a moment Madame Martin, like most of the French, is geographically challenged. 'Barbegal', she repeats, with another of those heavily disguised question marks.

'Yes, Barbegal. You know – the aqueduct'. Of course, once explained, Madame Martin understands the concept of Barbegal. Vaguely. In this, she's like many of her compatriots. It's another Jean Moulin statue moment: they've heard of it, but no-one's ever been. In truth, Madame Martin, momentarily forgetting she has to somehow get back chez elle, has reached that point in alcoholic consumption where, seemingly, nothing would make the day more enjoyable than a third glass of rosé. Monsieur Villiers has other ideas. Almost before our world class pickle purveyor has time to draw the next breath, the small vet from Plan d'Orgon has gathered up the baguettes, rushed into Casino to purchase charcuterie, a couple of tomatoes and a bottle of wine, bundled Madame Martin into the battered red car and driven off in the direction of Le Paradou.

Le Paradou is one of those places that are largely frequented by the ex-pats, especially in the winter months when there exists a need for soul-warming cassoulet. Generally speaking, Le Paradou is one of those places that sits next to somewhere more prestigious and thus becomes overlooked by the French. In this case, neighbouring Mausanne is far more in demand with its small but select art galleries and its square which is heavily populated with over-expensive bars. The ex-pats love Mausanne but so do the French film stars and politicians. Le Paradou, on the other hand, is off the road; off the track; hidden; almost missing. And another reason why it's frequented by ex-pats is because it boasts not one, but two English doctors. This knowledge is always handy following an excess of cassoulet. The only reason why the French-in-the-know might visit Le Paradou is to drive straight through and find a tiny, tiny back road that takes them to the Roman aqueduct at Barbegal. Even that's doubtful though: unlike the English, that lot on the other side of the channel don't tend to dwell on the potential celebrity of ruins (or the ruin of celebrities).

They jog along in the little red car in a comfortable silence. Madame Martin occasionally looks at Monsieur Villiers from the corner of a tiny eye. However, every time she risks a glance towards the vet, she finds that he is doing likewise in her direction. Inexplicably, this makes our pickle purveyor a little self-conscious and she passes most of the time looking out of the window. Madame Martin believes she has never previously traversed this very bendy road and in this, she is probably correct.

Madame is busy studying the woods which straggle down the hillside to her right. Because she is unaware that Daudet's windmill is hidden on the summit, she wonders where the tiny paths, edged by ready-for-the summer fire signs, might lead. Her reverie is broken by an announcement from Monsieur Villiers:

'Here we are, then'.

Madame wakes up and looks up. What should she see? Nothing, apart from a pile of stones on either side of the road and a curly blue arrow that's been painted on a tree trunk in a small lay-by. This is the Provençal equivalent of acknowledgement of a site of extreme historical interest. And when we say 'extreme historical interest', the rest of the intellectual universe means the greatest known concentration of mechanical power in the ancient world. Madame, overcome by mid-morning alcohol yawns. But Monsieur Villiers, a man of books and words, is on a mission.

He swiftly pulls the little red car into the small lay-by on the side of the lane. No car parks or visitor centres in this part of the world. With a plastic bag of refreshments in one hand, and Madame Martin in the other, our veterinary explorer takes his newly recovered old love onto the ancient track that runs alongside the remains of lichen-covered, once water-bearing arches.

'Pliny wrote about the flour mills', Monsieur Villiers informs his sweetheart by way of introduction to their environment. Madame Martin wonders whether Pliny works for *La Provence* and if he is the same Pliny who writes the weekend quiz and crossword. For the moment, she says nothing, trying to acclimatise to what is fast becoming an intense - given the time of year - sunshine-filled afternoon.

The old waterway, which may, at one time, have wended its way through a differently cultivated landscape, now gracefully divides large scale olive agriculture. It's difficult to surmise what might have been here in times past. The olives seem so apposite that something similar may well have existed for hundreds of years. Today, over-sized, brown and unexpected butterflies with frayed wings have also made an early appearance; whilst, overhead, the descendants of birds with gigantic wingspans float downwards from the Alpilles in a foray towards the plain, following the exact paths of their ornithological ancestors. Monsieur Villiers chooses his moment and his place as he lays the cheese and the tomatoes, the charcuterie and the bread and, of course, the wine, on a rug for today's pleasure. Alongside Madame Martin, he sits amidst antiquity and the two take their repose alone in historical splendour. And reader let's be clear, having come to terms with all of the morning's unexpected occurrences, and having allowed herself to be taken (emotionally, historically and geologically) back to the back of beyond, and having now found herself on a rug under an extraordinary piece of Roman industrial architecture in the middle of an olive farm, Madame Martin, like everyone else who has been lucky enough to discover Barbegal, is entranced.

Best to leave these two to their lunch, to their private conversation and to whatever else needs updating. Afterwards, they temporarily hide the residue of the picnic under the foot of an arch and journey along the remains of the watercourse to a point where they can look across the plain towards Arles. Here, they take in the vastness of the panorama and try to imagine what this place might have been like in times past. After this, each to their own, they consider what their own past time together was like. And after that, they walk back in silent time, collect their belongings along the way and Monsieur Villiers, reserving Daudet's windmill for another day, drives Madame Martin back to the top of the lane that runs away from the road between Noves and Cabannes. Madame Martin, having made no plans to meet with the vet in the near future, nonetheless, wanders contentedly back down the lane chez Martin, her very private mind full of wonderful new memories.

Chapter Fifteen

Although the ancient hen house has yet to meet with the newly cemented office floor, and thus become recycled into nothing short of a grand design, most of the recent upheaval chez Martin appears to have subsided. One evening,

Christophe is coerced into taking his papa to the PMU bar in Cabannes for dinner. Further, the partner who cannot be named has also been packed into the back seat of the pick-up truck. All of this would be normally unheard of on a number of levels. However, an almond-blossomed spring is still awaiting the arrival of summer and both Monsieur Martin and the partner need a break from kitchen stuff. Business at the bar being far from brisk, Monsieur le patron has, for a reasonable price, been persuaded to provide a small feast in the shape of several rabbits. Helpfully, his rarely seen wife, an unsuspecting prime candidate for one of those Swedish film noir narratives, has shot, daubed in mustard and cooked the bunnies before retiring upstairs to peruse particular internet sites.

Certain members of a fledgling cricket team have also arrived to share les lapins and make a few plans regarding forthcoming practice sessions and the meal has turned into something of an event. It's been decided that, in the face of no potential cricket venue, they will concentrate their efforts on acquiring all the necessary skills on the boules pitch in Cabannes. A proper wicket can soon be found once the weather turns, they feel. Previously, they have successfully avoided any attempt to learn the rules of cricket, having assumed that Christophe and Monsieur le patron of the Bar-Tabac in St Remy would doubtless update themselves and their team on the finer nuances of the game on the day. However, it seems that the partner who cannot be named has both researched the game and covertly observed the enemy to the extent that he is now regarded as the expert able to explain everything. The partner, therefore, being in great demand, has not managed to part with a French cent this evening and, given the amount of wine that's passed his way, is more than usually compliant.

He has dispensed a considerable amount of information. At first, most of it is greeted with disdainful laughter. However, once Monsieur Martin confirms that he has also personally witnessed the practice match over at Mas Saint Antoine, the gourmets decide that it might be profligate to approach forthcoming events with less humour. Let's be fair: there can be little serious about cricket but the well-being of the area depends on French glory. They've only just got over that tall Scottish bloke winning against Roland Garros; whoever he is.

Monsieur Martin is not much interested in cricket. Neither is he particularly happy at having to take his dinner so far from home. He's more concerned with the gymkhana. However, he's perfectly well aware that the evening will have more of a liquid theme than might generally be expected mid-week. Apart from ensuring that the small spotted ponies are comfortable and fed, he has nothing much to get out of bed for the following morning. The partner, meanwhile, having pragmatically acclimatised to something that bears no relation to his comfort zone, has no end of creative ideas on ways in which the ex-pats can be trounced. The partner has, under the influence of French bonhomie, forgotten that he is also an ex-pat. If he ever cared. A 'sort-of' plan is hatched. A 'sort-of' team is drawn up. As far as the partner is concerned, the overriding problem seems to be the refreshments: try as he does, he cannot make the others understand the concept of a cricket 'tea'. They know that tea is a drink to be avoided but cucumber sandwiches and scones have not yet invaded their parochial lexicon. Monsieur Martin reassures the gathering that, not a million miles away, there are sufficient women suitably qualified on the refreshment front. And anyway, Jean-Pierre Lucard will form a paella-laden rear guard on the day. As can be universally attested to in the business of decision making, the only way forward is to make a plan to hold a subsequent meeting and the evening, as far as anyone will be able to later recall, is deemed to be an unmitigated success.

The following Saturday, Monsieur Martin rises early and sets to on his courgettes, peppers and onions. The two bonnes madames have taken their pickles and jams on a trip to Arles. Gaining a site at this prestigious location has been something of a coup. It's one of the biggest Saturday markets in the South and stalls with corresponding venues have been passed down through families for generations: frequent visitors and even those tourists who only return every three or four years know exactly where to find their favourite olives or bread or fish. New entrepreneurs are rarely admitted. However, the burgeoning online reputation of those two is something that the commune elders would like a piece of and the women have, subsequent to the unexpected death without issue of one purveyor, been granted a two month trial.

Monsieur Martin takes full advantage of the peace and quiet. Lately, life seems unnecessarily challenging and it's good to get back to the prosaic. Summer is in sight and the length of the days is increasing: the sun appears at une bonne heure and its warmth permeates by ten in the morning. Soon, it will be hot by nine but, for now, the temperature is manageable. He tends his vegetables and afterwards looks to the well-being of the small spotted ponies. They've been busy and more foals are on the way. At half past ten, having completed more than a day's work, he stops for a cup of strong coffee and thinks about other days when Sophie would join him with the ponies. After this, he thinks of Gerard who used to whisper to the little ones and tell them the old stories of the Camargue. And after this, Myrtle Meades arrives loudly to organise the children who come to ride, and all the calm and pleasant reverie of the previous hours is tipped on its nostalgic equine head as Monsieur Martin is dragged back to the here and now.

Later, the two bonnes madames arrive home with extraordinary tales of success in Arles, greater than anything achieved at the yellow house. Christophe eventually drags himself from his post-Friday night bed and Myrtle Meades is invited indoors in the hope that something can finally be made of the gymkhana plans. The partner who cannot be named is currently sat on a wooden chair in his garden. He sports the usual mismatch of apparel, including a couple of towels that have, inexplicably, been wrapped around his neck. In one hand, he holds a glass of Sancerre; a gift of appeasement from Colin, yet another of Phyllida's ex-lovers who has come to stay from America after a forty year absence. Phyllida has little idea why she ever went out with Colin, who pronounces his name 'colon', let alone how he came to be in situ along the road that runs between Noves and Cabannes. The partner has chosen to ignore Colon since fifteen minutes after being introduced. The partner, who holds a hose in his other hand, has discovered a means of watering his plants that requires minimum effort apart from an appearance of total ennui sufficient to deter American ex-lovers with a limited vocabulary.

Monsieur Martin, beset by anxiety, calls over the fence to his friend and invites him toute de suite for impromptu aperitifs and input to event planning. On the way down the lane that runs from the road between Noves and Cabannes, the partner inadvertently secures the company of Phyllida who, despite her genetic hospitality, is now also anxious to hide from Colon. Louise and her husband, Ruud, who happened to be passing by, also join the gathering as does Richard Meades who's turned up to take his wife back home. Thus, unexpectedly, quite a crowd has gathered chez Martin determined to sort out the mess once and for all.

In a way, it's nice that things are meandering along in their usual fashion. On the other hand, however, Monsieur Martin feels that most of those meandering things are not in hand. Conversely, they are out of anyone's hand. And Monsieur Martin, simple though his life is, but not being simple himself, knows exactly why: 'there are too many things and too many people', he states to those gathered around that history-recording, decision-making table. 'If anything is to be made of the gymkhana and the cricket match, they must be combined', our not-so-simple host continues. The crowd gasp. Madame Martin has already dispensed the 'polite' aperitif which comprises a small glass of something offered to unexpected, and largely unwanted, visitors. However, her husband's declaration calls for something more substantial and an initial couple of bottles of rosé are introduced. Those gathered dutifully fill their glasses.

'It won't work', says Ruud. 'the feeling of competition between the cricket teams is too great to be hindered by a bunch of kids on horseback'.

Myrtle Meades is immediately up in arms: 'they're not a bunch of kids', she admonishes the Dutch contingent. 'They're the children of the village and their parents will want to see their tiny successes. And something for their money', she adds quietly. Her husband is on the side of the Netherlands' contingent: 'we want the cricket match to be significant in the battle with the French', he interrupts, momentarily forgetting whose wine he's supping. The French look at Richard Meades with an impressively consensual dislike. The situation is getting dangerous.

The partner who cannot be named, being astute and intellectual in nature, has ascertained his friend's objective: 'Monsieur Martin is correct', he announces and the gathering, recognising his astute and intellectual capabilities, turns as one to hear the justification and to demand more alcohol. 'Further', continues the partner, 'Madame Verte has written nearly 20,000 words of this sequel and we are no further on than we were when we started'. Everyone present looks around wondering who and where Madame Verte is. Madame Martin thinks, quietly, that the mysterious Madame Verte cannot be much of an observer if she's failed to notice that at least one of the bonnes madames is, geographically and emotionally, a bit further down the Chemin de la Liberté than during the winter months. She keeps this thought to herself.

Christophe dislodges himself from the meaningful table in order to fetch and serve more of the pink stuff. Monsieur Martin takes another swig: 'I suggest we hold the gymkhana and the cricket match over a two day weekend'. As more wine is consumed, those gathered agree that this might be a way forward. But which weekend they query?

'Well', says the partner, 'why not combine all known entities and plump for the Assumption of the Virgin Mary in August?' Actually, this suggestion is not that far removed from all things written in the cultural annals of French tradition. It's often the case that new events match the dates of ancient rites and rituals.

However, most of those present have not recently updated themselves with the cultural annals of France. Just as uproar is about to disrupt, there's a knock at the door. Reader, it can't be another important literary intervention because there's no-one left, apart from Colon, to make a timely intrusion. Christophe drags himself to the door, opens it, and finds a number of men from the PMU bar in Cabannes who have arrived with a small crane to move the hen house.

Chapter Sixteen

For a number of reasons, the two bonnes madames are in their elements. Firstly, and to rid ourselves of the quotidian, the new office block is finally in situ. That unrehearsed board meeting around the auspicious kitchen table temporarily progressed into a spontaneous party of sorts. And having established itself in its preferred form of amusement, the ambience then found itself the centre of a noisy reorganisation of construction. Because this is Provence, not a single eyelid was batted at yet another unplanned event and during the subsequent two hours, all the many participants who found themselves suitably lubricated to deal with potential disturbance naturally treated it all as par for the course.

The solitary venue at the bottom of the lane that runs from the road between Noves and Cabannes suddenly finds itself to be the epicentre of everything that is important in Provence. Kitchens and pickles play no immediate part. Somehow, those who possess no knowledge of domiciliary or international priorities discover that, on their unwritten list of parochial duties, the next big thing is supporting a neighbour in the construction of an office fit for the whims of women. Folk appear from all quarters to offer advice and guidance. Reader, understand, if you dare, that this is how things happen in the country. Aims, intentions and rationales are irrelevant: getting the job done is all that matters. It's the kind of philosophy that has held Provence together for so long that they've succeeded in building an aqueduct that remains the most important construction in the ancient mechanical world. For now, it's a hen house.

When the once-a-hen house and now-an-office is grounded, Madame Martin and Madame Lapin set to in organising mode. And have been arguing ever since. Madame Lapin has won the day and rightly so. Let's face it, she's the one who'll inhabit the joint. She's the one who's been dragged back into the corporate enclave. Madame Lapin *is* the one. Computers have been placed, wires have been traipsed, tape has been stuck, filing cabinets installed and flowers arranged. When Jean-Pierre Lucard visits, it's of vital importance that he finds Madame Lapin in an attractive juxtaposition of officialdom and femininity. If the vet from Plan d'Orgon ever comes this way again, Madame Martin will simply be grateful that he's found her. Any position will suffice.

Further to this, and in a more creative vein, the two madames have been charged with overseeing the refreshments for the gymkhana and the cricket match. This is more tricky. Ostensibly, it seems that some sort of coffee and gateaux followed by the paella purveyor is all that's needed at the more-difficult-to-cater-for cricket match. However, the partner who cannot be named has infused all and sundry with the necessity of providing an English tea during the sports event. Richard Meades has confirmed that this is de rigeur and Myrtle has offered to take charge. This intrusion is anathema to the pickle purveyors who can't be seen to lose face on the international refreshment front. All sorts of nonsense has brewed. Once internet connections were connected, Madame Lapin, who has every chance of failing in the blurred eyes of the chef from Orange, has been busy researching the contents of an English cricket tea. And she is confused and dismayed: how can a person place very thin slices of the hated cucumber between already-sliced bread and call it substantial? And what is cress? From where do they source small paper containers in which to put the contents of gateaux the size of Norwegian Blue feline turds?

And just as this turmoil is about to reach a boiling point sufficient to brew a proper cup of English tea, the end of March declares itself imminent. And with the end of March, come the municipal elections and the prospect of another six years' rule by the same Mayor of Cabannes who has been in post since time immemorial. Reader, this is an unchallenging account of rural life in Provence. Generally, we are not bothered by all things governmental even though our stories are set in one of the most politicised countries in the western world. And yet, because we are centred in one of the most politicised countries in the western world, it's important to be aware of trends that might have an effect on the plans of those who inhabit these pages.

Part Four

Chapter Seventeen

The would-be French cricket team have been 'sort-of' practising on the boules pitch in Cabannes. The accepted size of a boules court is four by fifteen metres. Therefore, whilst it's impossible to replicate a cricket pitch, this venue is reasonably sound in emulating a wicket. And the French team members are, at this moment in time, only absorbed in practising bowling, hitting and running. They're not captivated by fielding. Neither is the PMU team necessarily bothered by lost balls and broken windows. This bunch has cut to the chase and are in it for the accumulation of runs. They're getting quite good in small spaces. Unfortunately, there have been a number of incidents involving uninterested passers-by. Actually, the passers-by comprise most of the population of Cabannes and the doctor's surgery has lately been full of folk suffering bodily injuries of the sort emanating from assault by leather balls. There are more residents not in the team than there are cricket players. And several of the walking wounded have limped their sorry way to the offices of the mayor to make a complaint.

The incumbent mayor, Monsieur Mesquin, is preoccupied with the hustings. It's pretty certain he'll be re-elected at the end of the month: plenty of other folk dream of power but few want the time-absorbing inconvenience that comes with it. However, in politics nothing is a foregone conclusion: one never knows who's lurking in the legislative shadows with a back-stabbing knife to hand. Consequently, Monsieur Mesquin is more interested in a long-term set of false promises than the temporary wicket of minor injuries. The wounded complainants receive short shrift for their troubles by an equally shortsighted mayor who writes off this cricket fiasco as a trifling blip of no interest to the wider community. And in so doing, he makes a big mistake. The mayor thinks that cricket's an inconsequential problem. He's probably correct. However, misuse of the public boules pitch is not a minor transgression in the affairs of the commune. Currently unseen bandwagons are forming a protective circle around the grounds whereby defence might well evolve into attack.

To challenge the mayor, a person has to be a member of the city council. Inadvertently, since he previously oversaw changes to the established routine of the annual fête, preceded by the death of an ancient, Christophe fits the bill. Moreover, there have been all sorts of ructions down at the potato packing plant over the last year or so; not least of which has been the attempt by Cornish Earlies to unseat the indigenous varieties. Christophe has become something of a spokesman with regard to various rights of those born and grown in France. Challenges to those installed in that place we call Brussels you might say (although he couldn't possibly comment). Now, having recently moved from watching daytime quiz shows, and inspired by series one and two of *House of Cards*, this unlikely hero of the hour has decided to mount a last minute attempt to unseat Mesquin. It can't be that difficult.

Meanwhile, becoming suddenly aware of the disparity in numbers between men and women on the council, (actually, no women) Madame Lapin has adjusted her political awareness from zilch to bleeding heart liberal and submitted herself for municipal electoral representation.

Reader, how has this happened? Never in a month of sweltering Provençal Sundays could we have imagined this turn of events in our gentle and unbiased account of life in the

South. This is what happens when people erect statues and wall-paintings to local heroes that no-one, apart from a few partisans, previously knew about.

Madame Lapin has her reasons. She is a feminist of the first order. Well, maybe not the first but, like the aperitif, slightly late in the day, she's arrived there now. She has eaten from the jar of business success. She has seen how the St Remy cabal deride newcomers, yet made successful entry into the mosquito infected wetlands of far-more-important Arles. She has overcome the indignation of personal derision by men through kowtowing to the demands of threaded moustaches and silken stockings. She has, at great financial expense, purchased engraved jewellery for unrepentant, onion scented medallion danglers. And she is now forced to submit to pan-European ideals of cucumber sandwiches which are to be secondary to macho paellas. Anyone with an ounce of fortitude would say 'stuff this for a game of Camarguaise cowboys'.

And thus begins the briefest yet most frantic period of electioneering ever seen in the history of the universe.

Madame Lapin's platform has one supporting leg. It is the naked limb of gender inequality; specifically, that which results in sadness. She has made two interesting discoveries, one of which is that globally France sits below Ethiopia in terms of access to female political empowerment. Shocking as this is, she feels that her target audience, the women of Cabannes, will view the fact with apathy. Wherever a small commune in the South sits in relation to Ethiopia, wherever-that-is, will be of no consequence. Unknown to the wider world, the women of Cabannes are, largely, too miserable to care. Madame Lapin knows this from her own observations, from her personal up-and-down emotions, and from learning that

French women take more anti-depressants than any other group in Europe. And Europe being more geographically relevant than poor old Ethiopia, Madame has found a meaningful way to progress. In fact, Madame has identified the only thing that might garner interest and approval from the women of Cabannes: she will show them how to be happy.

In contrast, Christophe's short, sharp potential journey to the Mairie is along the well-trodden route to nationalism. One might argue that the goal was attained many years since. However, Christophe's ideology is more parochial in nature. He intends to bring tiny Cabannes into view by showcasing its superiority over the ravaging forces of intrusion. In short, the potato-packer will fight for a proper sports stadium in which to hold matches and tournaments. A stadium which will be the pride of Provence. A stadium to draw crowds from all over the country. A stadium in which the ex-pats can be beaten at their own games.

Chapter Eighteen

In an attempt to rid himself of all concerns regarding a cricket tea, the partner who cannot be named is once more secreted in a hidden part of his garden, his ears plugged by a brand new set of headphones. Colon recently departed for home, which the partner thinks is the best thing that the American did in the short passing of their acquaintance. However, before he left, Colon did something else which, initially, the partner thought came a close second to the previously mentioned best thing. Colon gave the partner a multi-layered gift. The partner who cannot be named is currently wearing a third of the gift on his head. Another third is being relayed through the headphones. The third is in the partner's hands to which, by way of explanation, we should proceed toute de suite.

The book in hand is written by a Bulgarian called Besino Duono. The partner is not au fait with this particular eastern European. Neither is he familiar with the strains that are permeating his ears. They have nothing to do with all that jazz, being more of a gypsy flavoured violin symphony. Nonetheless, the music is strangely haunting and the partner is not about to dismiss anything that emanates from his favourite culture. Supine on the Swedish chaise longue, he is amenable to almost anything that enhances his understanding of Bulgaria, a place to which he might have retired in another life with another person. Sadly, it takes only a short time before he begins to revive his hatred of the missing Colon. In fact, the partner is so appalled by the content of the literature before him that he starts to shout loudly in a variety of languages.

Colon, who spent more time with his hostess during his sojourn, has departed with a somewhat biased view of the partner. One in which our silver-haired protagonist readily attends yoga classes with all the prerequisite enthusiasm necessary for complete balance. Accordingly, and with all good intentions, the American has gifted, as they say in his illiterate part of the world, instructions for a circular dance to balance a man's physical, mental and spiritual forces. A dance to be undertaken every morning. The partner's physical, mental and spiritual forces are currently waging battle with each other. Paneurhythmy is not going down well.

Phyllida is close at hand. She has been busy with an electric drill, a saw and a number of wooden planks that have been ordered from the garden department of a Swedish catalogue. Phyllida is constructing a tree house for a grandchild that may or may not visit in a space between those times allocated for the holidays of past lovers she has quietly discovered on the internet. Actually, according to the instructions for assembly of the child's house, Phyllida shouldn't really be using either a drill or a saw. She chose this particular model, which is, or will be, replete with a miniature version of kitchens also sold in the Swedish catalogue, precisely because the marketing information claimed that the whole grand design could be completed by one person with one screwdriver and one hammer in six hours. Phyllida began work on this project at 9.30am. That is to say, 9.30am a week last Wednesday. Alerted by desperate calls emanating from the circle of willows, she pushes a way through reeds and branches to see whether her services are needed in departments other than those involving alcohol.

The partner is apoplectic: 'twenty eight movements', he yells at her. 'That colonic idiot', he continues by way of elucidation. But the so-called explanation is lost on Phyllida.

A number of Norwegian Blues have settled on the partner who cannot be named. The partner is very close to achieving that sense of spiritual balance wherein he would happily allow publication of his name if someone could only retrieve his sensibilities. Phyllida, surprisingly, has no prior knowledge of Besino Duono but feels this might be something worth looking into in a quieter moment. She rids her partner of Norwegian Blues, headphones, books and wooden slats, replaces him in an upright position and offers to bring a Mojito primed with garden mint. Phyllida is quite the expert when it comes to Mojitos. She's convinced herself that she can construct these cocktails without recourse to alcohol. She has grown a lot of mint precisely for this purpose. Just in case, there's always a bottle of white rum to hand. The bottle of just-in-case white rum is regularly replaced and Phyllida retains a constant sense of spiritual well-being even if the balance part is sometimes lacking.

The partner thinks a non-alcoholic Mojito laced with just-in-case rum might be exactly what le docteur would have ordered had he been consulted. In exchange, he readily donates everything related to Besino Duono into Phyllida's eager hands. Deciding, however, to keep the headphones, and now being two thirds free of Colon, the partner makes a move north from Bulgaria into Romania as the drums of Eugen Gondi soothe his troubled ears. In one hand, he holds a battered copy of his beloved Buddhist poetry. The other arm is bent slightly outwards with the hand open, although not in a paneurythmic style. The method of the one thumb, four fingers and twenty-seven bones in this appendage is one in which the art of waiting for a glass to clasp is well-practised.

Arms flapping, Phyllida consults her garden map and glides a happy way back to the safety of just-in-case bottles. Paneurythmic cats, noses held high, follow the protector of their physical well-being. Phyllida wonders whether Madame Martin and her partner might be up for a spot of early morning circle dancing. Accordingly, after the demanding felines have been attended to, and the partner's hand once more holds something useful, Phyllida, armed with the tape of paneurythmic music and the book by Besino Duono, skips down the lane chez Martin.

She locates the two bonnes madames in the hen-house-office where they are studying a pickle graph on the computer. Madame Martin, as usual, is cross but trying not to show it. No sooner had the bureau des affaires been up and running, than her business partner had disappeared into the electoral ether with her sights well and truly set on municipal glory. Try as she might, Madame Lapin is struggling to convince the other bonne madame that a week or so away from confiture sales will do no harm to the business. Au contraire, she argues, expansion is imminent.

'How do you work that out', Madame Martin demands?

Madame Lapin has a cunning plan. She will knock on every door in Cabannes and present the lady of the house with a free sample of jam or chutney. In this way, each household in the commune will have the opportunity to taste their wonderful produce and make it a regular purchase. Further, she continues, once installed on the council, she will have the power to ensure that the closed shop mentality of current market proprietors no longer extends to local French females who conjure products designed to engender well-being.

'Bah', exclaims Madame Martin. 'So now you're going to replace all the anti-depressants with pickle jars and women will be happy once again. Putain. You're in need of medication', she adds unkindly.

Madame Lapin tries to explain part two of her manifesto which involves all the women of Cabannes attending a newly formed discussion club in which they can voice the causes of their unhappiness. Madame Martin looks aghast but Phyllida, having made a timely entrance, thinks this last suggestion to have potential. Phyllida finds self-obsession quite rewarding.

'And I have just the thing', she adds. 'Could we lose the pickle chart and watch some paneurythmic dancing?' she wonders aloud.

There's a knock at the hen-office door. Everyone looks at each other and at the door through which Myrtle Meades stoops a careful entry.

'Mon Dieu', thinks Madame Martin to herself. 'We've got the full set now'.

To be fair, three of the women in the hen-office are not keen to watch an example of paneurythmic dancing of which, naturally, they know nothing. However, when Phyllida announces that the purpose of the morning circle dance is to make people happy, one of the bonnes madames takes an immediate interest. And by the end of the viewing, that particular bonne madame has added a new angle to her cunning plan. Moreover, Myrtle Meades, who has completely forgotten why she knocked on the door in the first place, is re-thinking the rarely mentioned gymkhana.

Chapter Nineteen

A long-forgotten and rarely used mobile telephone vibrates in the ever-hopeful, pickle-stained pocket of Madame Martin's apron. 'And about time too', she thinks to herself. Monsieur Villiers couldn't have chosen a better moment had he been a Kafkaesque fly on the kitchen wall chez Martin. Everyone she knows is busy with things that bear no relation to chutney and confiture and our dear Madame is beginning, yet again, to feel overburdened and unloved. To be honest, that day out in Barbegal might have appeased a lifetime's extra-marital needs but Madame Martin currently deems herself unnoticed by both the wider and nearer communities.

She looks at the text which, enigmatically, comprises one word: Gabriel. Madame Martin is at a loss to understand the message. Who the hell is Gabriel? She wracks her tiny brains and comes up with precisely nothing other than vague biblical references. Has she received a missive intended for someone else? Someone who may be called Mary? It doesn't matter: she wants to see Monsieur Villiers again; toute de suite actually. Using very small thumbs, she sends a reply agreeing to meet the following day at a point where the disused fruit-train track crosses the road between Noves and Cabannes.

So, on another promising (in more than one way) morning, with pickle problems to the rear, they meet at une bonne heure. The early sun's warmth already permeates the overhanging branches as Madame Martin, with little in the way of a greeting, climbs into the battered red car. In a comfortable and undemanding silence, these two adventurers wend a quiet way along secret lanes to who-knows-where. Well, presumably, Monsieur Villiers knows where.

Past the Pallas Cuir, on the road to Arles, they take an unexpected turn to the left. Madame Martin is temporarily taken with the building to the right which, like a vaguely Pisan relative, is leaning in a worrying way towards Arles. She fails to notice that Monsieur Villiers who, let's face it, is the only person in the South aware of the primordial history of Provence, has made a subsequent motorised right angle left into an uncompromising lay-by. No curly blue arrows here. Nothing, in fact, to suggest what's up-and-coming. These two insignificant-beings-in-history leave that old red battered car behind and walk towards another of the best-kept secrets in this part of the discarded world.

Madame Martin is truly shocked and enchanted by the beauty of the ancient olive grove before her. She feels as though she's walked up three or four inconsequential stone steps and been immediately transported into a spiritual time and space that defies any attempt at categorisation. Monsieur Villiers is a past master at removal of and from the quotidian. As if nature, geography and biblical history had not already completed such a sufficiently splendid display, somebody, in the name of art, has strung gossamer hammocks between the gnarled tree trunks. The hammocks contain the yellow oil of the olive through which the mid-morning sunbeams dance a sparkling farandole. In this once-in-a lifetime display, the grove shouts out its mysticism and Madame Martin counts all her blessings on tiny fingers. She is unaware that the greatest secret has not yet been disclosed.

Reader, you query the earlier biblical reference? In the middle of all this joy stands St Gabriel's Chapel; its façade covered not only in the graffiti of other visitors from other centuries, but in strange evocative carvings that demand a latter day code-breaker: Daniel is trapped in the lions' den; Mary receives an important annunciation from the eponymous Gabriel; Adam and Eve undertake an afternoon in their garden and so on.

'But what does it all mean?' Madame Martin asks her own private historian as she sits, entranced, on a little, who-knows-how-old stone wall. And Monsieur Villiers proceeds, like Aladdin's lamp, to permeate yet another timeless environment with his own brand of magical illumination; for here be dragons. Well, one dragon in particular – a fearsome creature known as the Tarasque. Thus does our dear Madame learn the reason why the beautiful chapel was built here in the apparent middle of nowhere on the site of another edifice that existed in the days when monsters roamed the land. It's true that folk in this tiny part of the cosmos still hold a great and important secret linked to Chappelle Saint Gabriel. Does Monsieur Villiers know the secret? And does he share it with his chérie?

There is one thing that Madame Martin certainly knows: no matter what twists and turns her tiny life takes, the unassuming vet from Plan d'Orgon can be relied upon to transport her, in all senses of the word, to places where nothing but the moment matters. They walk along the side of the chapel and Monsieur Villiers points out a small opening in the stone wall where the enormous black bees of the South have formed a dark cluster of business in the intense heat of this day-to-be-treasured. And afterwards, in a would-be habitual manner, Monsieur Villiers spreads the blanket of love beneath the lichen-covered trunk of a hundreds-of-years-old olive tree.

Chapter Twenty

The troops have gathered under the leadership of Commander Christophe, potato- packer extraordinaire, who speaks for the people. His people. Some of the soldiers are dispatched on a mission to deliver the manifesto through all the expectant letter boxes of Cabannes. Others are busy knock-knocking on village doors, demanding a representative presence at tomorrow's meeting at the PMU bar. This latter strategy is optimistically mapped out with a selection of brightly coloured pins on a battered chart of the commune. But, this important political document, pinned to a cork board on a wall of military HQ in the room above the aforementioned venue, indicates results are proving unexpectedly tricky. Christophe, who has taken a week's sick leave from the potato plant, is facing repeated returns of the musketeers bearing reports of mutiny.

'They want to know what we're giving them', explains Michel.

'We're giving them glory', the leader responds.

'Not enough', Michel retorts. 'They want to know where their gift is'.

'What bloody gift?' the commander demands. 'This is France. We're the most politicised nation in Western Europe. We despise the ex-pats. We're in it for national and local pride'.

Michel, like all the other soldiers, falters: 'bien, certainement, but how will you match the pickle?'

Power, it seems, depends on whether the macho troops reach the doors of the village before the opposition; and whether the person that opens the door is male or female. Because, if Madame Lapin's soon-to-be-happy helpers reach the residence first, and are greeted by a desperate-to-be-happy housewife, polls indicate that gifts of chutney and jam are winning the race.

'Putain', explodes the Commander in Chief, 'can't we give them a baked potato? Or a plate of those delicious cheesy chips?' The troops are aghast:

'But cheesy chips were invented by an ex-pat cricketer', they reply in horror. Although, secretly, each holds a private yearning to, right that moment, and any other moment, devour a dish of the corrupted potatoes.

Thus, this hither-to politically aspirant competition for the unresearched common good, has somehow degenerated into a battle between male sport and female happiness. So, no change there then. The only positive point in all this political mess is that Christophe and Madame Lapin have hit respective nails bang on their heads: unlike most who have fumbled a power-driven way before, at all levels of political desire, these two novices have succeeded in identifying exactly what it is that drives the would-be electorate. The trouble is, that in so doing, they've manage to divide the community in half.

There are ructions in almost every household in Cabannes: families who, up until this point, have assumed the nightly traditional positions of those in charge of the remote control and those banished to the kitchen, are up in arms. Wives no longer speak to husbands. Husbands who, let's face it, seldom ever spoke to wives, are left to starve, whilst the women of the village are not only busy communing with each other at all hours, but are collectively dousing every single meal with unnecessary pickle or jam as if to make some sort of poisonous point.

Christophe sits ruminating on a plastic chair outside military HQ with a bottle of beer. Having dismissed his sentinels, he is having a rare quiet moment which lasts about three minutes. This is all the time it takes to reach the only possible decision: abandoning the beer, and reader, we know this indicates the seriousness of the situation, the potato packer jumps into his purloined pick-up truck and travels, toute de suite, down the road that runs between Cabannes and Noves until he reaches that dusty old lane. Is he going chez Martin to sulk? Of course not. Christophe is going to seek advice from the partner who cannot be named.

For once, the partner is not hiding in some foliage-ridden, secretive part of his ever-expanding garden. It's nearly the hour of the aperitif and in expectation of passing visitors, Phyllida and the partner are seated with the Norwegian Blues on their patio. Mint-driven, infused with just-in-case white rum, Mojitos are in evidence. Pleasing Bulgarian strains emanate from the remise where a musical ensemble may or may not be gathered. Phyllida is not sure who might turn up for this early-in-the-year soiree so she is delighted when the dirty pick-up truck screeches to a halt outside the boundary fence and Christophe stumbles into their other-world. Phyllida, in practice for longer and warmer evenings ahead, rushes into her new kitchen to retrieve another glass, more ice and a small dish of those herb covered olives.

The would-be mayor sits on an unwelcoming chair from a Swedish catalogue and recounts his political problems to the partner who, despite knowing everything, cannot be named. As ever, the partner dispenses extremely serious but apposite guidance:

'Drink at least two just-in-case Mojitos and absorb the Bulgarians', he advises.

Clearly, this is sound counsel and Christophe feels reassured. Life has been far too hectic lately and he needs a reason to sink back into the South. And just as the potato packer is managing to relax, a semi-naked man, previously intent on driving past on a tractor, spots an unchallenging aperitif and also departs his vehicle outside Phyllida's gate. And Christophe, who, let's face it, is struggling a bit, is unexpectedly surprised to share a drink with his father.

Reader, you have already spotted the obvious which the potato packer seems to have missed: Madame Lapin and Christophe are competing for two different roles in the political history of Cabannes but, in so doing, their intentions have become temporarily entwined.

'Why not entwine them further', suggests the mint-infused partner? Christophe is a little confused.

Well', continues the partner, 'you and Madame Lapin aren't seeking the same office. However, you've both identified and succeeded in alerting the good folk of Cabannes to exactly what's missing in their lives. But, in so doing, you've divided them'.

'Exactement', responds the potato packer. 'The woman is trouble'.

But what', says the canny partner, who would like his dinner sooner than later, 'what, if you joined forces? What if she became your running mate?' Christophe, who knows better than to be foiled by a Swedish chair, downs his extremely just-in-case second Mojito and straightens his back. He looks at his semi-naked father.

'Bien sur', intervenes the tractor driver with a film director's astuteness at intervention. 'The woman's a bloody nuisance but she knows how to get things done'. The deed is done which is more than can be said for the gymkhana that might never happen.

Chapter Twenty One

Monsieur Mesquin is relaxing in his office. Glass in hand, his fattened calves fit for a possibly prodigal son, plus his swollen ankles, loved by the mosquitoes of the South, and his rather-too-large feet that have abandoned all thoughts of political footwear, are resting on a red faux leather chair when his chief of staff falls through the door with upsetting news.

'Monsieur, le gracious maire', bows and curtseys the sycophant, 'news from the arena'. Monsieur Mesquin is unmoved: 'are the toilets blocked again', he asks? Monsieur Mesquin is otherwise occupied with a glossy magazine in which politics are conspicuous by their absence.

'Mais non', replies Gaston. 'The bullring has been commandeered by the French cricket team. They are bowling and running and catching and hitting pieces of wood'.

'But', Monsieur Mesquin astutely observes, 'surely this is good news? Doesn't that mean they're no longer upsetting everyone on the boules course?' discretely closing his reading material. 'And who cares anyway', he thinks secretly'.

'Mais, non', the excitable and excited Gaston continues. 'It means we can't go ahead with tonight's bull fight'.

The venerable mayor, in the well-practised way of those who consider themselves venerable diplomats, venerably considers this news. 'Are there observers?' he asks politely.

'Mais, bien sur', reports Gaston. 'Hundreds of them', he enthusiastically continues with just a hint of exaggeration.

'Well then', surmises the mayor, 'it's a splendid opportunity for me to attend and give a pre-election speech. And afterwards, we'll clear the wickets and bring on the bulls'.

'Mais, Monsieur le maire', Gaston explains. 'You don't understand: some of the observers are supporting the cricket team; some of them are there to argue for a new stadium; and some of them', he falters, 'are there because they refuse to be in … their kitchens', he finishes quietly.

Monsieur Mesquin, who doesn't quite understand either the content or implications of any of the preceding conversation, studies his naked feet. He takes a nothing-in-moderation swig from his glass and concentrates on his big toes. The mayor is rather disappointed with his feet. He feels they don't really seem to match either each other or what they're carrying, in terms of stature. He sets to with the paper knife, carving away like a modern-day Rodin. On the left side, he slowly fashions a dangerously pointed claw. The flunky inwardly cringes. Monsieur Mesquin, symmetrically intent, approaches the right. 'How does this affect my presence?'

Gaston, on a number of levels, is appalled but feels it's in his interests, as chief of staff, to explain. He averts his eyes from the ornamental pedicure. 'Monsieur le maire', he bravely forges on, 'no-one in the bullring is interested in anything you might say. It's a revolution'.

Monsieur Mesquin raises a bushy eyebrow and a beady, piggy little eye peers out through the overgrowth. Monsieur Mesquin's eyebrows are well-known in Cabannes. Some unkindly types have been known to comment that one strategy the mayor could employ to cosmetically disguise his bald head would be to comb his eyebrows back over his skull. Even harsher inhabitants of the village have gone further in suggesting he could layer the hirsute entities protruding from his nostrils downwards to form a moustache of sorts. No-one has yet combined lengthy ear hair and sideburns in a single sentence, but that time cannot be too distant. 'A revolution you say', repeats the less than attractive mayor. 'Is that all? Not very imaginative for the French. Next, you'll be telling me other would-be candidates for my red chair will be addressing the serfs with a theme of fraternity and liberty. And equality', he adds, choking on the last of those three nonsenses. A silence, heavier than the mayoral insignia, falls over the office.

'What?' demands Monsieur Mesquin.

'Well', Gaston continues cautiously, 'there is a small rumour that the potato packer and his running mate will speak to the people'. He backs away, anxiously making a mental note of the distance between the desk and the office door.

'What!' Monsieur Mesquin jumps to his naked feet and takes a step or three towards Gaston. The artistic but lethal toenail on the left foot stabs the unprepared and swollen right ankle. The ankle and the air are blue in response.

'Call up the troops', demands the mayor. 'We're going to the arena toute de suite'.

....

Reader, we have made a necessary, but irritating, quantum leap into the excesses of political endeavour. Such is the way with aspirations of and to power but, in terms of generally slow moving Provençal life, there are huge and unexplained voids. To be fair, with only ten available days of campaigning we have to cut short the narrative: more important things like cricket matches and gymkhanas and love affairs warrant our time but still …

… Christophe, having been advised by a range of folk, including his father and the partner who cannot be named, bravely visits the bijou apartment of the once feminist librarian. To say this is a shock for all concerned would be an understatement. At the time, Madame Lapin was entertaining the paella purveyor from Orange. Somewhere in her busy schedule, Madame Lapin has made an essential space for her ever-complaining lover. Both parties have one simultaneous eye on their respective mobile phones: Jean-Pierre Lucard, in case he gets a better offer, either in terms of people needing a paella or women needing a man, but, hopefully, both; and Madame Lapin, in case she gets news of political importance: in other words, a preferable turn of events for these two followers of the 'get it when you can' philosophy. Medallions are swinging and hairless legs are clamped when Christophe knocks on the door.

'Ignore it', instructs the breathless paella purveyor.

'Could be someone important'. Madame Lapin notices the irritation in her lover's eyes. 'Someone politically important', she continues unsteadily. 'Someone who's hungry', she

94

falters. It doesn't matter: the moment, like many others recently, is lost and Jean-Pierre Lucard is already buttoning his shirt. Partially.

Enter the would-be mayor who, to cut a long, boring and unnecessary tale short, á la mode of the not-very-meaningful love-making, persuades his mother's business partner that political success requires hitherto unanticipated alliances. Madame Lapin takes little persuasion.

And this is how a bull-fight that has been side-tracked by a cricket practice is overtaken by a political rally of, as yet, undetermined importance.

Chapter Twenty Two

The partner who cannot be named is under the cover of the willow, busy watering that part of his garden which borders the place where diseased pear trees once bravely stood. The small spotted ponies have been brought in from the field alongside the lane that runs chez Martin and are currently enjoying the early evening shade offered by the few remaining trees. Monsieur Martin, fresh from his own watering chores on the courgette and pepper allotments, is wandering between his herd on the other side of the fence, muttering disconsolately to Cabut and Hebdo when the partner espies him.

'Everything ok Henri', asks the person who is a little one-sided in the realms of first name terms? Monsieur Martin nods sadly but without conviction.

'How about a glass of something', suggests the partner, discarding his hose-pipe? 'Why not pop round? Phyllida's doing something essential in the kitchen and there are no other guests', he explains with some relief to both parties. No sooner said than done and minutes later these two are sat on the terrace with nothing more important between them than a chilled carafe of white wine and the company of Clovis. Due to the presence of this latter guest, Norwegian Blues are absent from the aperitif. Within the remise the Bulgarians strike a comforting musical accompaniment but they are shortly to be subsumed by the shrill tones of a telephone. It's of no immediate concern to the two neighbours who are, as ever, in denial of outside intervention. The day is winding down and the cicadas are, like our dear Monsieur Martin, also giving in to anything that has hitherto sustained them. The partner who cannot be named doesn't press his friend for an explanation of downheartedness but, like us, he knows how that first sip of goodness can change demeanour one way or another.

'I think the vet has returned', offers Monsieur Martin by way of uninvited explanation. This apparent elucidation is lost on the partner who, if he ever knew, has long since forgotten men from Plan d'Orgon.

'Are the ponies sick?' he enquires.

'No. I mean Monsieur Villiers', continues his neighbour.

'Ah', replies the partner, although it's clear he has no recall of the possible relevance of this statement and has little idea of what might usefully be added to the conversation. The frog chorus commences from the ditches on the other side of the road that runs between Noves and Cabannes and Monsieur Martin sniffs in a manner that has nothing to do with hay fever.

'She's up and down like a fiddler's elbow', he bravely continues.

'Madame Martin', the partner reasons. But just as the scenario reaches a stage where the whole sorry history might be recounted yet again, Phyllida arrives fresh from the telephone, surprisingly minus olives, ice and alcohol. The two men and the wolf-dog are amazed at this history-making absence of auxiliary refreshment.

'That was Louise,' she reports. 'There's going to be a disturbance in Cabannes. Shortly'. The Bulgarians, having resumed the upper hand in audible accompaniment, forge on as if nothing had ever interrupted their pleasantries. Clovis snarls for good measure and promptly resumes reflecting on private plans for his new family. Monsieur Martin feels vaguely perturbed. However, depending on his neighbours to quickly deal with any aperitif-intervening problems, he takes another sip of life-affirming wine. But the partner who cannot be named is irritated to a hitherto unseen rage. Just as he's trying to offer unconditional support to the only man who's ever given him a willow tree, the apparently ridiculous person to whom he remains an unnamed partner arrives with incomprehensible, nonsensical news.

'What do you mean, there's *going* to be a disturbance?' he demands. 'How do you know this? What type of disturbance? Where are the gendarmes?'

Phyllida is taken aback by the vitriol and, reader, understandably so. This is the man who sits on a chair with towels around his neck reading sixth century Buddhist poetry. This is the man in Provence who exudes the ultimate in calm (as long as no-one mentions paneurthymy). This is the man who, now we come to think of it, becomes irritated quite frequently at all things directly or indirectly related to Phyllida.

In cosmopolitan mode, Chinese whispers have shimmied their Provençal path along the narrow alleys of Cabannes, up and down the roads and through the telecommunications that link the village with the outside world. Well, the world immediately outside Cabannes. Never before have the good citizens of the area witnessed a live political rally. It's not quite an electoral frenzy: they're in it for the novelty factor, but only on condition that events are terminated in time for bulls to enter stage right.

'Well', retorts Phyllida, 'you two can stay where you are but Louise and Ruud are on the way to take me down to the village'.

Monsieur Martin attempts a pacifist's intervention: 'if you don't mind, I think I'll give it a miss'.

'Are you sure?' asks the partner of the partner who cannot be named. 'You do realise that your son will be speaking against Monsieur Mesquin?'

Quelle horreur all over Monsieur Martin's little brown face: 'That imbecile?'

'Which imbecile?' asks Phyllida? 'The mayor?'

'Non', a distressed pony breeder responds, 'Christophe!'

The partner who cannot be named, following his initial annoyance at intrusion during the aperitif, adjusts his perspective. He is, after all, an intellectual and nothing of local political importance has ever happened in all the time he's lived in Provence. Further, in case you haven't already guessed, dear reader, the partner has latterly become a reluctant closet admirer of the potato packer and his aspirations.

'Mon ami', he suggests gently to his friend, 'I think we should go. Could be history in the making. Could be something to tell your grandchildren about'.

Monsieur Martin nearly chokes on his wine as he shudders at the thought of his only son and heir producing offspring but he is reluctantly persuaded to support Christophe. After all, at one of the many previous aperitifs, he vaguely remembers encouraging the boy to join forces with his wife's business partner.

'Shall we collect Madame Martin?' enquires Phyllida. 'It seems that Madame Lapin will also be on the platform'.

As far as Monsieur Martin can recall, there is no platform in the arena. There are circles of seats, a circular fence and a circle of grit on the floor on which potentially virile, but largely pubescent young men wage war on bulls. There are a number of boards between the fence and the circle of grit over which young men in danger can leap and hide from unexpectedly bad-tempered bulls who are fed up with the entertainment business and who would rather be grazing peacefully on the Camargue.

 'Don't get Madame Martin', he remonstrates without elaboration. And just as decisions are made, the most important of which is to abandon the aperitif, Louise and Ruud turn off the road that runs between you know where, pause outside Phyllida's place long enough for political voyeurs to embark, reverse, and speed off towards the arena.

Meanwhile, Madame Martin, she who feels generally excluded from life, remains in her lonely kitchen. She is boiling and peeling, scraping and chopping, sieving and bottling. Of course she knows about events in the village: Chinese Provençal whispers intrude on the most doomed of locations, including those down dusty lanes. But Madame Martin has little interest: events may be significant, she thinks, but the next big thing is always only just around the corner of individual lives. And, she concludes, significance is a transitory illusion. Madame Martin is quite the philosopher on the quiet. She looks at the saucepans of bubbling chutney, thinks about missed opportunities, removes a sticky mobile phone from an apron clad hiding place and with deft little thumbs sends a slightly suggestive text to a vet.

Chapter Twenty Three

Earlier that day, Jack Shaker and his lads have a team meeting, unexpectedly at Charlie O'Connor's place. They begin with a late lunch in the Bar-Tabac des Alpilles with a view to discussing match plans. They choose this venue because it's a convenient half-way point between anywhere and home. It's also handy to go to St Remy on any day barring Wednesdays to pick up their dry cleaning, get a quick haircut and purchase a copy of yesterday's Daily Telegraph. Of course, up-to-the-moment news is always available on the internet, but it's not the same as reading comfortably biased accounts of events and affairs.

Proceedings have begun well enough with a couple of light beers and a discussion of the previous evening's football results in the land they now refer to as 'the old country'. As Jack once said, 'we're hardly likely to call it 'home' again unless Britain decides to leave Europe'. How they'd roared.

Harry Larwood notices that today's plat du jour is entrecôte and frites with a blue cheese sauce. As they all like this type of French cuisine, the team decides that they might as well eat there. And this involves a couple of carafes of rosé from the Ventoux which loosens a few tactic-talking tongues. Normally, this wouldn't matter. Practice at Mas Saint Antoine has been going reasonably well but the start of Ruud's summer season is imminent and the team has to find another location. Further, there's a sense of something lacking – unity perhaps – which is why Jack Shaker and Buddy have called this meeting. However, somewhere towards the end of the steak and chips, at a point where the possibility of an Iles Flôtant is becoming a desirable probability, Jack calls an unexpected halt to business.

Monsieur le patron of the Bar-Tabac has been in attendance throughout: hovering and serving and waiting and being generally helpful. The ex-pats take this personal attention for granted being as they are, important customers. Even so, Jack finds it rather odd that their table hasn't been assigned to a subordinate. Monsieur le patron must have better things to do with his precious time. It suddenly occurs to him that walls and patrons have ears. The thought that their friend and host night be a mole is upsetting and Jack immediately dismisses the idea from his mind. But that nagging little doubt is not to be spurned so easily. It keeps returning to lurk around various cerebral corners until Jack can no longer ignore it. The suggestion that their match strategy – if they have one – might be stolen, sold and dissected by others is too risky and he calls for the bill.

'But I was going to have a floating island', whines a distraught Harry Larwood. 'You hardly ever see them these days'.

'Me too', agrees Richard Meades. 'They're thin on the ground now they've been deemed old hat by Parisian tourists'. And in a flash, the whole team is decrying the denial and demise of raw egg in runny custard and the lack of coffee. It's difficult for

Captain Jack to explain his reasoning without upsetting Monsieur le patron who, after all, might just be interested in their well-being.

'It's necessary that our plans are kept between ourselves', he informs his colleagues. The team members look blankly at the detritus on the table. Then they look around the Bar-Tabac, wondering who else can possibly be interested in their conversation.

'Who's bothered about our plans here?' asks Dickie Sparrow.

'Well, you never know', replies Jack, raising a vague eyebrow in the direction of Monsieur le patron. For a moment, no-one understands the code but, with the most precision the team has ever shown, all as one turn their heads in the direction of the Frenchman. Monsieur le patron turns his head to look over his shoulder. For the last twenty minutes, he's been trying to follow the conversation but with little success. At one point in the not too distant past, he had the distinct impression that there was about to be a bulk order of Iles Flôtant. This was alarming as only last night, the momentous decision had been taken to finally stop serving the dish despite the fact that the Bar-Tabac des Alpilles was now the only joint in town where such a delicacy could be purchased. As it happens, the floating island moment passes out into deep water and Monsieur le patron believes he must have totally misunderstood what was going on.

Shortly after this, Monsieur recalls, Captain Jack asked for the bill before making some other comment which resulted in the entire team turning to look at him. Monsieur le patron, thinking that something untoward is happening behind him, turns to look over his shoulder but in the exact same second, he suddenly realises he's been caught out. 'Meh bah', he thinks, 'it's of little consequence; this bunch don't seem to have a plan between them'. All the same, Monsieur le patron is hurt to think that some of his best customers believe he might be spying. Especially as he's learned nothing of interest and has failed to sell any non-existent deserts or coffee.

Charlie O'Connor's moved house again. He sold his first home and is now on his third rented property. Nothing seems to suit him or, if it does, it fails to agree with his perfectly formed wife, Sarah. They've been living out of cases in rooms full of largely unpacked boxes for about four years now. Charlie's got his desk and computer set up in one of the many bedrooms. Sarah's got her clothes hanging on a rail in another. There are lots of books scattered about the house apart from in the bathroom. The bathroom is the only part of their residence that looks as if it's serving the purpose for which it was designed. White towels of differing sizes lie waiting in neat bundles. Bottles and packets of expensive toiletries fill two shelves along one wall. A marginally smaller shelf on another wall houses ridiculously priced, but essential-to-maintenance cosmetics. To the side of Sarah's basin sits one of those horrifically magnifying mirrors that Madame Lapin possesses, a shiny jar of cotton wool balls, a carved wooden box from Mexico in which velveteen tissues reside, and a beautiful candle (Scent of the South) aboard an engraved silver saucer. To the side of Charlie's basin is a cloudy plastic tumbler holding a misshapen tube of toothpaste and a sprouting toothbrush.

Charlie has everything he needs, which is mostly Sarah. Sarah has all that she needs. One of these days, if they stay here long enough, she might attempt a spot of interior decoration elsewhere in the house. Might. She has no interest in the kitchen. In this respect, she's about as far removed from

Phyllida as it's possible to be. Thus, to say Sarah is horrified when, around 2.30pm, Charlie turns up with an entire cricket team in tow, would be an understatement. She is appalled and follows her husband into the seldom-seen kitchen where he's gone to look for some wine.

'Have you got any nibbles?' asks Charlie genially.

'Have you got any brains?' she responds. 'When did we start to do nibbles? There might be a tin of tomato soup', she adds helpfully, trying to change the tone of her voice. 'Or a packet of Custard Creams'.

'Don't worry', he tells her kindly. 'We've had steak and chips. Just thought it might be worth asking'.

'Shall I come and entertain?' Sarah continues with no idea of how this might be accomplished; and is hugely relieved to learn that this won't be necessary. She pokes her coiffured head around the living room door long enough to say 'hello'.

'Hello', reply the cricket team members who have distributed themselves on, around and in an assortment of boxes.

'Goodbye', says Sarah, backing out of the doorway.

'Goodbye', says the cricket team.

And surprisingly, the well-oiled team has quite a good discussion regarding plans and tactics and strategies and suchlike for at least two hours. Well, until the time that Jack Shaker's mobile phone rings. Jack looks at the phone.

'Ruud', he informs the player-spectators. Jack listens to the messenger and addresses his men.

'We'll have to call a halt to business,' he instructs them.

'What, again?' comes the response.

Captain Jack continues: 'we have to go to the arena in Cabannes. Apparently, the French cricket team have been spotted practising there'.

'Bloody hell', exclaims Charlie, 'what about the bulls?'

Jack hasn't considered the bulls. 'It's an opportunity to watch the other side that we can't afford to miss'.

'Really,' yawns Dickie Sparrow, 'it's already been a long day and the aperitif is calling'.

But Jack is adamant and goes on to relay news of something of political importance that may be happening at the arena later. The men are bewildered to hear 'political significance' and the little village mentioned in the same sentence but, with some reluctance, the now somewhat bedraggled team gird their collective loins and set out once more, this time in the direction of Cabannes.

Chapter Twenty Four

When everyone departs the patio at Phyllida's in such unexpected, aperitif-wasting haste, Clovis is rather taken aback. No-one has thought to invite him along on their devil-may-care adventure. In fact, Clovis is pretty sure that no-one has thought anything about him. He follows the troupe through the jasmine-swamped gate and onto the lane. He watches them as they clamber into Ruud's shiny black car but they leave without so much as a wave or a turn of the head.

'Ha, ha, not so special after all', says a blue furry monster that has crept up behind him. 'What are you going to do now then?' Clovis knows full well what he'd like to do and offers a snarl-of-sorts.

'Oh yes', asks the monster, 'looking for some action?' And it raises its four-humped back. Luminous blue fur spikes itself along various ridges like a band of marauding Mohicans. Clovis knows better than to pick a fight in which he will probably be the sorry loser and backs off in the direction chez Martin.

'Going home?' enquires the band of Mohicans. 'Not going to visit the kids then? What's left of them'.

Clovis stops slinking and stands very still. 'What do you mean, what's left of them?'

'Oh, didn't you know?' taunt the Norwegian Mohicans. 'They're all going to new homes. 'Better say bye-bye toute de suite', they mock.

Clovis is mortified. But Clovis is also very, very angry. The Norwegian Blues don't anticipate a response and it's precisely because of this that they're rather wrong-footed when the wolf-dog pounces. To be fair, Clovis hadn't foreseen his actions either so he is equally surprised to find himself rolling around the dusty ground with a number of felines of foreign origin. It's a brief, bitter and noisy affair, the sounds of which reach a kitchen without an island down the lane. Madame Martin is busy studying the pickle-clad mobile telephone. She looks up briefly, is unable to identify the source of shrieking, squealing and snarling, and looks back expectantly at the wretched means of mobile communication.

Poor Clovis can't remember the last time he saw Nanette and the children. Ever since he intruded on the ex-pat cricket practice and stole a red leather ball, all his usual points of entry into Mas Saint Antoine have been boarded up. Perhaps the evil Norwegians were lying, he thinks. But even they couldn't have invented such a dreadful fallacy. Somehow, he must discover the truth. He turns off the dusty lane and wanders through the remainder of the pear orchard adjacent to Phyllida's place. Charlie and Hebdo, also forgotten by Monsieur Martin, are under the trees and they nod to the wolf-dog in passing:

'Off for a stroll?' asks Hebdo genially.

'Going to look for my kids', Clovis replies without stopping.

'Bon courage', Charlie neighs.

Clovis spends a lot of time sniffing around the Mas Saint Antoine perimeter fence looking for a way in. To begin with, it seems like a lost cause. His last point of entry had been by the mimosa bush which has long since shed its blossom. Someone has mended the gap in the fence with a new piece of chicken wire. Other erstwhile access places are likewise blocked. Clovis looks up and notices the back of the shed where Ruud keeps the mowing machine and where the fence ends. It looks too tight for a wolf-dog. Clovis breathes in, shimmies along the wall and out onto the neatly mown lawn of Mas Saint Antoine. For a moment, he sits quietly and looks around. Then he spots movement under a bank of oleanders. It's Nanette and three of the puppies. Just as he's about to rush over, she spots him and offering a bark of delight, runs to the shed, puppies in her wake.

Everyone is thrilled to see everyone else and they spend some time running around in circles, chasing tails and noses. The puppies, who of course are much bigger than the last time we met them, are not very sure who Clovis is. However,

Maman is happy so they are happy even if the visitor is very large.

'Chérie, where are the other three?' asks Clovis. The jumping and chasing and circling stops. Nanette looks sad.

'They've gone to new homes', she reports. 'Louise says there are too many dogs here'. And the story becomes sadder as Clovis learns that only one of the remaining children will be allowed to stay with its mother. Homes are being found for the other two.

'Merde', cries Clovis, 'c'est terrible'. He thinks for a moment. 'I know', he decides, 'I'll take one of my sons now and hide him'.

'It won't work', says Nanette, 'they'll find him'.

But Clovis is adamant. He won't be able to make a choice so he closes his eyes and grabs the nearest puppy by the scruff of the neck.

Chapter Twenty Five

Everyone's been busy setting out to somewhere or other. Mostly, they're all heading in the direction of the arena in Cabannes, although one has gone off to the neighbours' place. People from Plan d'Orgon are not, however, going in either of those directions. Largely, people from Plan d'Orgon are staying home as they always do, fearful of abuse from the rest of Provence. Monsieur Villiers is an exception to the rule. The curly-haired vet has received a late-in-the-day text from the outside world and is in his old red battered car heading towards a dusty lane. Monsieur Villiers, who always seems to be ready to answer any command that Madame Martin chooses to send his way, arrives promptly. Business has been slow today at the veterinary surgery in Plan d'Orgon and even if it wasn't, this seems a better offer although he's wary of encroaching upon the homestead so late in the day.

When Monsieur Villiers turns down the well-trodden dusty lane that runs from the road between Noves and Cabannes, there's little to indicate who might be lurking chez Martin. The field is empty of ponies and there's no sign of welcoming wolf-dogs. The pick-up truck is missing but this means little as he knows Christophe sometimes takes it on his small travels. Semi-naked men are also conspicuous by their absence so the vet parks the battered red car and attempts a tentative knock on the door; which, owing to her fortunate proximity to that infamous entrance and exit, Madame Martin happens to hear. Just.

'Monsieur Villiers', she says on opening the entrance to love and life, 'you'll have to knock harder than that if you want to remain a part of this story'. Reader, this isn't what she said. Why would she be so formal after all that picnic-blanket interaction? But, let's face it, we've come so far and still don't know the first name of the vet: there's only so much we're privy to.

Monsieur Villiers assumes he's taking his chérie somewhere or other. These two are always going to or coming from secret assignations. It's a transient relationship in as many senses of the description that you can conjure. But Madame Martin has other ideas. She's sick to her tiny back teeth of always having to travel miles to spend time with her paramour.

'Let's have a glass on the patio', she suggests.

The invitation, which is really more of a command, startles Monsieur Villiers. It's about as unexpected, in both a real and literary sense, as a proper knock on the door. It would be difficult, for example, to imagine the person from Porlock receiving such a greeting. Further, the vet from Plan d'Orgon is not even aware that a patio exists chez Martin. And this lack of awareness is well-founded: the presence of something resembling an aperitif-supping terrace at the end of this lane is as likely as an island unit in the kitchen. Still, Madame Martin, two glasses and a bottle of rosé clasped adeptly in her miniscule hands, is already on her way through the back door to a point where two rickety garden chairs sit on a place once occupied by overgrown rhubarb. They're not really garden chairs: they're wooden chairs that once lived in the house and have been thrown outside.

And to be truthful, the rhubarb is still in evidence, rhubarb and ginger confiture being a best-seller. However, the would-be path that Madame Martin used to fight her way through in order to feed Clovis in the bad old days is not the overgrown troublesome route of the past. Christophe, in one of his rare productive moments, cut back the brambles and created at least the semblance of somewhere to sit on warm Provençal evenings. Not that many people chez Martin take the opportunity of sitting outside but still, it's a comfortable nod in cultural and meteorological directions. Madame Martin is happy enough. Monsieur Villiers, on the other hand, displays signs of anxiety:

'Should we be here?' he asks restlessly. Madame Martin explains how the politics of the day have resulted in everyone they might feasibly know being, at this moment, in the arena at Cabannes.

'But what if they come back?' enquires the nervous vet. Madame Martin is aware of the first signs of irritation she's ever felt towards him.

'Well, they won't', she snaps, topping up the glass of Monsieur Villiers.

And the vet decides to try and relax. After all, it's in no-one's interest for him to be found behind chez Martin enjoying a few glasses of rosé with the lady of the house without good reason; so he engages Madame Martin in cultural conversation as though this was the sole purpose of a just-passing-by visit. In particular, the tiny vet from Plan d'Orgon has a desire to visit Les Alyscamps in Arles with his lady friend on their next outing.

'It's a Roman cemetery', he explains.

Madame Martin, who is still not quite certain what she wants from her liaison with the vet, but is sure it's not a picnic with skeletons, responds with a withering look. Monsieur Villiers tries to offer some historical and cultural insight to the necropolis. Madame Martin looks bored. She's a bit behind with the chutney and confiture and is hoping that this evening will be an entertaining diversion; not a soliloquy on the dead of Arles. The trouble is that being taken somewhere unexpected in the Provençal countryside is far more pleasing in practice than a lecture on archaeology.

'Shall we go shopping in Avignon?' she suggests.

Madame Martin never goes to Avignon. Avignon is a twenty minute drive away but it might as well be another country in somebody else's life. Madame Martin has no clue what types of shops the city might boast and even less idea concerning possible purchases. Our dear Madame has been steeped in the Provençal countryside for so long that she is accustomed to life without luxury. A fancy cosmopolitan restaurant inside the ancient walls, for example, doesn't feature in any list of desires she may have ever privately made. Half a bridge across the Rhône, laden with tourists, has as much attraction for her as an evening at the arena. Conversely, some bread, cheese and wine under an arch of the aqueduct at Barbegal is far more enticing and adventurous. Reader, don't mistake Madame Martin's lack of enthusiasm for the safety of a simplistic comfort zone: we know she's not entirely satisfied with life at the end of a lane. But the city holds no truck for her. So why did she make her suggestion?

Poor Monsieur Villiers is considering exactly the same question. He's been wrong-footed at every turn this evening and can't understand what mistake he's made. He thought he understood Madame Martin's needs on all levels. And, mostly, he does. The current problem has only ever been identified by one person: Madame Lapin and her platform of female happiness. It's just one of those things. And Madame Martin, a little ashamed at her frankly unjustified behaviour, tries to repair the evening as she fills up the glasses, looks at the setting of the orange sun and listens to the dying song of the cicadas.

'I'm sorry', she says. And she is. And so are we but we don't know how to help her.

'Would you like to talk about what will happen to us in the future?' Monsieur Villiers asks. He's not thinking about outings. He's thinking about whether there will ever be anything more than a relationship that develops and dies and starts again. Madame Martin knows this but is not ready for a discussion, the outcome of which, she's sure, will determine her future existence in Provence. She feels that Monsieur Villiers deserves an answer that she's unable to give. Madame Martin hopes there will be a timely knock at the door. There isn't. There's something else entirely unanticipated. Just as she's about to confide a possibly life-changing decision, their attention is drawn by the arrival of a wolf-dog with a squirming animal clenched in its jaws.

'Clovis', shouts the pickle purveyor. Clovis, startled and stopped in his homeward tracks, looks around with a guilty expression on his face. 'Merde', cries Madame Martin, 'what's he got? Is it a rat?'

The vet jumps up and moves towards Clovis: 'mais non chérie. It's a puppy'.

At the same time that Monsieur Villiers springs into veterinary action on the hitherto unknown patio, closely followed by the chutney creator, a number of people fall through the back door.

Chapter Twenty Six

When the political observers from the road that runs between Noves and Cabannes arrive at the arena, they are quite astounded: it's as though the village is en fête. The canteen outside the enclosure is thronged with pastis-swilling crowds. A separate, make-shift table has been speedily set up further along to hold red wine and plastic tumblers; thus dividing one set of preferences from another. Men of all persuasions gather in large groups around each bar, thereby creating a slightly threatening crush as they form and reform like huge amoeba. However, bonhomie is much in evidence with jovial kissing and meaningful handshaking.

The sad women of Cabannes stand aside, arms folded, watching the men of the village love each other. The sad women of Cabannes have already undertaken their ritualistic sizing up of each other's waistlines, counted each other's wrinkles, compared each other's outfits; have vied to be the one wearing the tightest jeans and generally preened their neuroses. But when the sad women of Cabannes have finished with all this half-hearted nonsense, and turn to look at the men, there is an almost-hint of epiphany in the air. The arena is some distance from the road that runs between Noves and Cabannes and is currently, on a philosophical level, leading more in the direction of Damascus. All they need is a gentle conversion.

Phyllida surveys the scene and suggests to Louise that Madame Martin has missed a trick. That little stall over there, where a budding fourteen years old entrepreneur is busy unloading cartons of second-hand tricolours, could have been a chutney distribution point had anyone possessed any forethought. She wonders where Madame Martin's business partner has gone. Not far, actually, but out of sight in a tiny changing room that has been temporarily commandeered as a political HQ for her and the other half of her dream ticket. The other half is conspicuous by his absence. Christophe is, of course, down amongst the real men, laughing and joking his way to political endearment.

Madame Lapin had hoped that Jean-Pierre Lucard might have squashed himself into the HQ changing room to see her prepare for a possible moment of glory. When Madame Lapin decided to represent the sad women of Cabannes, and when she agreed to be a partner on the dream ticket, it hadn't occurred to her that she might have to address a political rally. Alone. She could do with some support in the departments of emotion and confidence. It's a false hope. Jean-Pierre Lucard is also, after all, a real man and is, therefore, amongst the others at the Pastis counter. Had there been advance warning of the size of this gathering, he would have prepared an impromptu paella stall. That's the trouble with politics: every time you think stability is rife, democracy rears its troublesome head. He's quite cross at what seems to be a succession of missed opportunities and is determined to follow the election closely over the next few days.

The wickets having been cleared, the grit having been raked and the teenaged toreadors having been preened, the crowds are called into the arena. They take their seats noisily, full of enthusiastic expectation of who knows what. A blast from the warning siren calls them to order and from inside her hidey-hole Madame Lapin hears a huge cheer go up. Two lavender coloured nails peep round the slowly opening door and the lady of the moment carefully leans a half-coiffured head out. The first thing she sees is Christophe standing on the other side of the arena, microphone in hand.

'Merde', thinks the running partner, 'I should be out there with him. He could have come to collect me'; which, of course, does not epitomise the usual sentiments of an independent feminist politician. Madame Martin is unsure of what to do next. If she goes out now, she fears she will detract from Christophe's glory. If she stays put, she'll miss her chance. But Christophe starts speaking to the crowds and the moment is lost.

There's no doubt about it, Christophe has come a long way since the days of watching TV quizzes with maman. Maman has also come a long way, although not as far as the arena Christophe notes. Still, the old man is there. Onwards and upwards. Christophe speaks eloquently to his people. The people wave their second-hand flags. He speaks of nation and state and of the state of the nation. He speaks of village and commune, of young and old, of tradition and change. He speaks of the bravery of the French cricket team who have mastered a new and alien game in order to be the best at this as well as everything else. Amongst the male sections of the crowd, there isn't a dry eye in the house.

Jack Shaker and his men were stopped earlier from entering the arena on some flimsy pretext of health and safety. That they never saw the French cricket practice is of little concern: they'd assumed the official had concocted the feeble excuse to save the opposition embarrassment should anyone see how bad they are. Now, however, the ex-pats are taken aback by this apparent lust for sporting blood.

'Bloody hell', observes Charlie O'Connor, 'this could get nasty'.

'Shush', glare his near-to-hand French onlookers, 'the leader is speaking'. And Christophe is, indeed, in full flow once more. He points out the shame in having to defeat the ex-pats in a bullring. He reminds his people that there's no stadium for their sport-aspiring children to practise in. And he explains that, with each citizen of Cabannes paying just one extra euro every month in taxes, a shiny new stadium can be constructed. The crowd boos. The crowd hisses. Christophe is taken aback. He hasn't expected such vitriol for one euro a month. But from her political spy-hole in the changing room, Madame Lapin can see the source of the crowd's distress. It isn't Christophe and his one euro stadium: it's Monsieur Mesquin who has just entered the arena.

'Bloody hell', says Charlie O'Connor, 'it's going well'.

Relief floods over the potato packer as he finally notices the maire. Christophe lifts his evangelical arms high and commands silence from his people. The flags droop in the dying sun. Monsieur le maire is horrified at what's unfolding before him. He must make the speech of a lifetime if he's to reclaim any sort of civil stature. He gives it his very best shot. At first, the crowd is disinterested and restless but crowds are fickle entities. Especially when they're under an illusion of democracy and the effects of Pastis. Gradually, Monsieur Mesquin, relying on old-fashioned politics, picks a few niggly little holes in Christophe's crocheted ideology. In particular, had the maire known that each adult was willing to part with another euro a month, he would've suggested a new school and theatre years ago. The ideological blanket unravels as the crowd begins to perk up.

'Bloody hell', says Christophe, 'where's that bloody woman?'

He calls Madame Lapin sur le telephone. 'Where are you?' he demands.

'In the HQ waiting for you', comes the response. Christophe reckons the maire has had sufficient time to talk and, snatching the microphone, he once gain demands silence.

'Mesdames and Messieurs, the final speaker is here. I give you Madame Lapin'.

The hitherto quiet, sad women of Provence go mad:

'Lapin, Lapin, Lapin', they chant.

'Moutard, Moutard, Moutard', someone responds but is soon kicked into touch as Madame Lapin finally makes her entrance onto the political stage. She stands resolutely next to Christophe, wipes away one of those famous stray wisps of hair from a bright eye and begins to speak. The crowd fall silent which is just as well because, at first, the business partner and running mate speaks firmly but rather quietly.

'Speak up', someone yells. Christophe leans over, turns up the volume on the microphone and suddenly the message of happiness screams across the arena making everyone jump.

'Bloody hell', says Charlie O'Connor, 'calm that woman down'.

Madame Lapin locates the optimum tone and volume and continues with her plan for the well-being of the women of Cabannes which, in turn, will lead to calm for the men. The men yawn or snigger and are generally restless and Christophe is anxious. He might have made a mistake in joining forces although he can see that the women admire his running mate.

Chapter Twenty Seven

Eventually, it finishes. In truth, no-one is any the wiser: all the candidates have been surprisingly impressive but no-one can please everyone for even some of the time. It remains to be seen what can be accomplished in the forthcoming days. It's just a tiny bit anti-climactic. Madame Lapin is emotionally exhausted and looks around in the hope of spotting the paella purveyor. Jean-Pierre Lucard is also looking around but not in the direction of Madame Lapin. The man from Orange has undergone something of a revelation this evening although not one that relates to Madame Lapin's political and oratory skills. No, what has really surprised Jean-Pierre is the discovery that there are so many unhappy women to hand. In a generous and magnanimous frame of mind, he's wondering how many of these sad ladies he might be able to help out of the doldrums.

Monsieur Martin and the partner who cannot be named have had quite enough culture for one evening and both are missing the aperitif.

'Come to the PMU bar', suggests Christophe. 'We'll review our position'.

Monsieur Martin and the partner who cannot be named do not want to review their position, or anyone else's come to that. They would like to regain their previous position on a terrace with a glass of wine to hand. Further, Phyllida is anxious to get home and polish some olives; Louise and Ruud have also been sufficiently entertained in political departments for at least several months.

'Well', says a slightly disappointed Christophe, 'why don't we all go chez Martin for the aperitif then?'

Everyone, for different reasons, is aghast. It's true there have, occasionally, been unplanned events that involved alcohol at the bottom of the lane, but never has there been a formal invitation for the aperitif chez Martin. Monsieur Martin is particularly perturbed:

'Where shall we all sit?' he enquires. 'It's too hot for the kitchen'.

Christophe doesn't bat an eyelid. 'We'll sit on the terrace', he replies.

Papa is even more confused: 'what terrace?' he demands.

But Christophe is adamant that they'll simply remove some chairs from within and sit outside the adventurous front door. 'Plenty of room out there', he reminds Monsieur Martin. The gathered assembly considers this option. It could be a bit crowded amongst the pick-up truck and the chickens and all the other detritus of life chez Martin. Largely, however, they're polite enough to keep their considerations to themselves. Phyllida thinks it will be fun and anyway, Christophe seems a little sad that they don't want to go to the PMU bar.

'We could go to our place', Louise suggests in a last ditch attempt to instil some order on proceedings. But Christophe is on a mission: he's got a plan and he wants to put it into action.

Monsieur Martin has one last try at halting a party at his tumble-down homestead: 'What about your mother?' he asks Christophe. 'She's not going to be very happy when we all turn up there unexpectedly'. It's a good and justifiable move.

But Christophe will not be swayed: 'rubbish', he argues, 'she's been there all on her own with the saucepans all day. She'll be glad of the company'. Thus, the motion is carried. Two or three of the aperitif-driven party briefly look for Madame Lapin but she is nowhere to be found and, feeling that they are sufficient in numbers, they pour themselves into a couple of vehicles and head off in the direction of the road that runs between Noves and Cabannes.

Part Five

Chapter Twenty Eight

As we have seen, there is a sense of unfinished business after the rally in the arena. Most of the French contingent couldn't really care less what happens now as long as bulls are involved. The sad ladies of Cabannes begin to disperse. They are reasonably inspired by Madame Lapin's speech but are unclear how their lives will be changed, let alone improved. They don't want to return home and start preparing dinner; neither do they want to remain with their sweaty spouses. The sweaty spouses stay behind as a mutually adoring group to watch the even sweatier bulls that have at last been granted access to the arena. The bulls and the men are hot, bothered and grumbling, all of which bodes well for the evening's action.

The bulls of the Camargue are well aware of the difference between their lives and their Spanish cousins who are called upon to perform in the grand arenas of Arles and Nimes. The bulls of the Camargue spend their lives with the gardiens and know these men well. They know their idiosyncrasies. The bulls are well aware that, when they enter the arena, it's fair play and no-one will die. Conversely, when their Spanish cousins enter the ring, it will be a ritualistic and shocking fight to the death. Reader, I'm saying nothing except that Camarguaise bulls that have been kept waiting in political wings have every chance of getting the better of adolescent razateurs.

Jack Shaker and his lads are not interested in bulls. It's been a long day one way and another and they regroup around the Pastis bar with a view to returning to their various abodes. Surprisingly, there's a Frenchman at the canteen who also has little interest in what's happening in the arena. Some of the cricket team members know Jean-Pierre Lucard and view him, it has to be said, in some awe. Reputations travel fast in a place where everything else, apart from traffic and lovemaking, moves slowly. Incidentally, the latter only applies to the French as the sad women of Cabannes, and indeed the rest of their female compatriots will confirm. Urban myths usually comprise rural reality.

Despite his interest in locating sad women, Jean-Pierre, being a man who revels in his own charisma, is full of bonhomie towards the ex-pats. He doesn't boast a great deal of English it's true. However, once they discover that he is the chef extraordinaire in the department of paella, they are more than interested in holding some sort of discussion regarding the cricket match refreshments. Jack Shaker feels that engaging a Frenchman to provide the evening meal will impress the opposition and go some way to making up for the loss that Team PMU will surely suffer on the day. When Jean-Pierre becomes aware that the ex-pats have no idea that he's already been booked for the sporting occasion, and despite a deal having already been arranged with the French side, has no qualms in offering a new and extra arrangement to his new friends. Never let it be said that the man from Orange is not cosmopolitan.

Having struck a provisional financial deal with Jack Shaker, the paella purveyor suggests they all remove to the PMU bar where arrangements can be clarified and confirmed over a glass of well-being. Authentic it may be but it's not the most salubrious of venues. Further to feeling that they might have experienced all that Cabannes has to offer today, most of Jack's lads are finding it difficult to remember the last time they ate anything of substance. However, they don't want to offend the man from Orange. Richard Meades has a suggestion: why don't they all take Jean-Pierre to Noves where they can enjoy a simple meal with a carafe or two of wine at La Plancha? This idea is met with great enthusiasm by one and all; several intend to phone their wives with instructions to meet them there.

Thus, in no time at all, a convoy of vehicles has gathered in the car park. At the head, naturally, is Jean-Pierre Lucard on his quad bike, medallion glinting in the last of the day's dying sun. Just as they're about to depart, Madame Lapin comes running around the corner, delighted to have finally located her errant lover. In truth, the errant lover fails to look as happy as he might at this reunion. Nonetheless, he understands that many of his new friends will be meeting up with their own women over in Noves so, wiping the disappointment from his handsome face, he instructs Madame Lapin to climb aboard and clasp him tightly: a command with which the independent political candidate standing for the happiness of women is happy to comply.

Thus, this enthusiastic, if slightly wilting parade processes along that infamous route. Some of the more energetically soaked amongst the group peep and toot their horns as if attending a wedding which they are happy to claim no part of. All of which means, that in attendance of the noisy quad bike, they completely miss both the lane that runs from the infamous road and any sense of disturbance emanating from its conclusion. Which is just as well as there are more than sufficient folk experiencing a slight surprise chez Martin.

La Plancha isn't expecting such a demanding crowd. It matters not. La Plancha is in Noves and nothing has ever upset the people of Noves. Let's be honest: nothing has ever upset a restaurant in the South. Jean-Pierre stalks in as if he's been a patron all his life and within minutes a table has been assembled for twenty people. The wives and girlfriends of the cricket team are, upon instruction, ready and waiting to join the party. They are suitably adorned in various states of finery: bronzed shoulders bare, ears bedecked with sparkling jewels, feet enclosed by high-heeled sandelabra. The man from Orange is in his element and chooses a seat next to the loveliness that is married to Cheesy Chips O'Connor. And Charlie's wife, despite an earlier desire to be anywhere but here, succumbs instantly to onion-scented charms.

Madame Lapin, relegated to a side-show at the end of a bench, glares at the proceedings. Our dear librarian who is fighting for the happiness of women is in feminine turmoil.

Chapter Twenty Nine

Another party has recently departed the arena in Cabannes. This party is not as noisy as those who will shortly travel to Noves for steak and chips. In fact, many of those going chez Martin are more than a little anxious regarding their destination. However, having already undertaken unanticipated diversions from the normal course of events at the end of a day in March, and this being an evening that bodes well meteorologically, this lot are sufficiently keen to relax in the company of the re-visited aperitif. There are no tooting horns to accompany their progression along the leafy road that runs between Cabannes and Noves; thus, there are no audible signals to alert people taking an unexpected drink on a previously non-existent terrace to what might be in heading their way.

Vehicles arrive chez Martin with occupants ready and primed for a glass of rosé to be taken in the very last embers of the dying sun on a hitherto unknown patio. Vehicles spill their occupants onto the end of a dusty lane in the middle of nowhere. Occupants expect to be greeted by the pickle purveying, solitary lady of the house who will surely be pleased with the unexpected company. Madame Martin is conspicuous by her absence. But the cicadas are bravely singing their finale. One or two passengers, namely those who reside chez Martin, notice the presence of a small red battered car. Friends and neighbours, who fail to be alerted by small red battered vehicles, are unaware of the symptoms of alarm raised by those who live here. Guests simply tumble through the normal detritus, enter a front door without the usual requisite literary knocking, lurch through a mediaeval kitchen devoid of islands and, as a shapeless group, fall through the back door.

Some members of this party are pleasantly surprised to discover an aperitif-welcoming terrace, even if it's surrounded by rhubarb infested foliage. Some folk even grab a kitchen chair on their way through. Monsieur Martin and his son are not quite as content with what they find outside. For a start, there are two half-full abandoned glasses and the remains of a bottle of the pink stuff. Further, and more disturbing, two small people seem to be rolling around amongst the scrubland. Even though the two small people are covered in dust and grass and are in a generally unkempt state of affairs, they are instantly recognisable as the lady of the house and an unseen-for-quite-a-while veterinary practitioner from Plan d'Orgon.

Apart from a suggestion of previously unnoticed and currently unseen snarling and yelping, it would be fair to say that almost everyone chez Martin is rendered speechless. Voices shortly return:

'Bonsoir', from the partner who cannot be named.

'Can we help?' from Phyllida who is greatly disturbed by the apparent lack of herb covered olives.

'I'll search for more glasses', from Louise who is stepping backwards into the kitchen.

'Monsieur Villiers, have you ever played cricket', from Ruud who wants to be somewhere else. Ruud knows that he is expected to do something interesting with two duck breasts this evening. The two duck breasts should, at this moment, be relaxing in an exotic marinade and not feeling cold and unwanted in a freezer at Mas Saint Antoine where they were hastily dispatched once news of political disturbance in Cabannes came through. Actually, as that was their second visit to arctic climes in one day, the likelihood of them ever safely appearing on a dinner plate is now non-existent. Ruud picks at the olives disconsolately. Like Phyllida, he wonders how anyone could ever dream of serving a black olive devoid of herbs.

Reader, I can't report the words that are uttered by Christophe, the would-be mayor, who had hoped to initiate the first in a series of politically inspired hospitality events chez Martin this evening. Christophe dives into the scrub with the intention of attacking and seriously damaging the vet from Plan d'Orgon. However, as in the bad old days, a wolf-dog emerges from the rhubarb-infested foliage and lunges at the candidate's throat. Monsieur Martin, a man who has been emotionally challenged beyond anything that might be vaguely regarded as acceptable, and who, until this point, has remained in a state of shock, suddenly moves forward, driven by paternalistic instincts to save his son. And the partner, who cannot be named, with all the predispositions of a man intent on the continuation of the aperitif in the company of his willow-donating friend, grasps his neighbour by the scruff of the neck and thus prevents untimely damage. Or death.

Reader, in real life, all of these things occur in a chaotic millisecond. Other people present say other things: some hurtful, some explanatory; some irrelevant. The time that passes is so brief that the cicadas are still chattering, the frogs have not yet commenced singing and the owls are yet to awake. Naked olives have miraculously been coated in herbs as they sit on a tiny dish on an ancient cast-iron table. Bottles of icy rosé also adorn the table-top. Sufficient chairs have been located to house all of the rear quarters of all of the people chez Martin. It's the simple and necessary apero that annuls all past grievances. Feelings are still hurt but tempers have been subdued as information of political achievements is subsumed by news of a kidnapped love-child.

The French, especially those that live down a lane that runs from the road between Noves and Cabannes, are probably the most polite people in the universe. Monsieur Martin, unable to bear the company of the Provençal elephant on the terrace, wanders off to make sure the small spotted ponies have sufficient water to see them through the evening. And there can't be visitors in any other part of the known world who are more accepting and unquestioning than his cosmopolitan friends and neighbours who have made a home in this fruit producing paradise. Phyllida nibbles happily on an olive. Ruud reconsiders the line-up of the ex-pat cricket team. Louise, who, let's face it, has more than enough to deal with at Mas Saint Antoine, sits quietly on a rickety kitchen chair gently stroking a tiny puppy on her lap.

'He needs a name', she announces. 'How about Gabriel?'

In a moment that passes so quickly that no-one else notices, Madame Martin and Monsieur Villiers glance at each other. Monsieur Villiers would like to celebrate the choice of name but keeps his own counsel. Madame Martin would very much like someone to tell her what she's supposed to do with her life. She would like to follow her husband into the remains of the orchard and offer some sort of life-affirming apology. Madame Martin would like the vet to leave. Madame Martin would also like the vet to stay. Forever. In the meantime, however, she agrees that Gabriel will come to live at the end of a dusty lane that runs from the road between you know where.

Louise continues: 'Ruud, we should keep the other two puppies'. Ruud, sensing a potential compromise regarding the frozen ducks, agrees without hesitation. And under a patio table that few had ever known existed, Clovis whines.

Chapter Thirty

It's the middle of another July. Saturday afternoon. The blistering sun is beating down but is unable to make any impact on a tall woman wearing a hat fashioned on an oversized sombrero. Myrtle Meades, busy in the paddock chez Martin, fully clothed in white linen drapes, resembles a kind of fungus. Not one of those expensive types from the truffle market at Carpentras, but a more anaemic, alien type of growth. The sort your parents warn you to avoid. The little children who attend the miniature riding school are, of course, also clothed in protective headgear. Somewhat more surprisingly, the little children are also wearing what appear to be matching white linen drapes. From the air, the scene probably resembles a mysterious giant albino toadstool and all its spores. But this perspective, and indeed the one we might witness from ground level, is incomplete for there are others present just out of immediate eye line. Reader, you may anticipate the mention of Monsieur Martin here who, of course, initiated the miniature riding school. However, you would be wrong. For Monsieur Martin, who possesses nothing in the way of white drapes and who, further, has no desire to own anything especial in the department of wardrobes, is currently to be located behind chez lui.

Past the rhubarb foliage, in an area that has long since been cleared of undergrowth and overgrowth, Monsieur Martin is busy harvesting another crop of misshapen but sumptuously colourful courgettes and peppers. In this, he is being helped by one and a half wolf dogs: Clovis and his son Gabriel are doing their utmost to lend a helpful paw. Not that long ago, Monsieur Martin wouldn't have dreamed of leaving the village children and the ponies with Myrtle Meades but, although Provence tries its very best not to change, some progression has to be made. After all, there's no point in having a hired hand, unpaid though they may be, and doing the job oneself; especially if a gymkhana that wasn't envisaged in the first place has evolved into something far stranger.

Who else is in the paddock, also clothed in white drapes? Bearing in mind the aforementioned sartorial relevance, we can immediately discount the partner who cannot be named. Whilst he adores the small spotted ponies, it's on condition that they're viewed from another side of the fence that partitions the place where pear trees once stood defiant in the face of disease. Further, having been coerced into the role of cricketing counsellor over the past eight or nine months, the partner has no inclination whatsoever to become embroiled in equestrian entertainment. It's bad enough that, amongst other things, he's turned into some sort of sporting fashion adviser to the French: folk in the white cotton business are having a veritable heyday in these Provençal parts what with cricket and mysterious drapery. No, the partner is out of sight in his high summer, splendorous garden, employed in the serious matter of seasonal dead-heading.

There is, of course, a distinct possibility that Phyllida would be up for a spot of white clothing of the non-cricket variety but, at this moment, she's busy in the nearly-new kitchen with a number of prawns and a clutch of chillies. The only bird's eye view in her nutritional aviary is the wall clock on which a different bird marks each hour with a matching squawk. The never-seen-in-Provence herring-gull has only just startled Phyllida to the fact that it's not much longer until Mojito-o-clock. She looks around anxiously for the mint. And the rum, in case it's a just-in-case day which, inevitably, it will be.

Reader, it's not even worth considering the remote possibility of Madame Martin being in the paddock, let alone being clothed in any kind of impractical white-wear. May I remind you that it's Saturday afternoon. That's the afternoon that supersedes Saturday morning. And with their earlier forays into the market at Arles being an overriding success, the two bonnes madames now have a regular Saturday morning chutney and confiture stall in that ancient town of Roman ghosts. Following their drive home northwards along the currently sunflower-lined road, above which, today, Bonelli's eagle was spotted, the other bonne madame disappeared; but Netty has helped an apron-clad Madame Martin unpack a few leftover goods and prepare the peaches and apricots ready for today's sugaring and boiling. Monsieur Martin will shortly arrive with the latest crop of chutney related vegetables from the kitchen garden. There's no time for either ponies or vibrating pockets on a sweltering Saturday. Nonetheless, despite various missing persons, Madame Martin is not as cross as she might have previously seemed. Business is still booming but, more importantly, the kitchen chez Martin, separated forever from office-type affairs and incomprehensible technology, is finally refurbished in such a way as to make pickle production almost effortless.

So, perhaps a reformed Christophe currently accompanies the small spotted ponies? Let's face it, he sadly has little else to do on a Saturday when the potato-packing plant is closed. It was always going to be difficult transferring this story into one that was primarily concerned with politics. And poor Christophe fell at the last mayoral hurdle whereupon the incumbent candidate became, once again, the secular high priest of Cabannes. It was a good contest and one with which the folk of Cabannes thoroughly engaged. They loved the idea of a competitive upstart fighting Monsieur Mesquin for the crown but the challenge was, in itself, sufficient novelty for these parts. Traditional paternalism must rule when it comes to overall leadership. And Mesquin was in a position to offer greater support to a wider range of people than Christophe could ever hope to.

On the other hand, some change was embraced. Reacting perhaps to their husbands' insistence that the unattractively parochial Mesquin should remain in charge, sufficient members of the electorate, of whom we might suggest the majority comprised the desperate housewives of Cabannes, voted Madame Lapin onto the council. Hurrah! And, as in the general history of life, all it took was the promise of happiness. Thus, one of the two other persons present in a paddock is none other than the contentment-seeking first lady councillor, now also clothed in white drapes. Reader, where to begin with an explanation? How about Nebraska, USA?

A long time ago, a man from that irrelevant state, having perused one of those internet sites that offer a chance of hope with past failure, journeyed up and off the road that runs between Noves and Cabannes. And having hit that dusty lane, he immediately turned through a jasmine drenched gate into Phyllida's place. Further, probably having outstayed his welcome by about three weeks, Colon departed, leaving behind music and literature relating to all things paneurythmic as a gift to the partner who cannot be named. You may remember that, in exchange for a non-alcoholic Mojito, primed with a spot of just-in-case white rum, Phyllida took paneurythmic ownership. And following this convoluted state of affairs, and with, it must be said, more than a degree of suspicion, the white-clothed early morning dancing subsequently became something of a necessary, if secretive, ritual with Myrtle Meades and the small spotted ponies, and Madame Lapin and the desperate housewives.

All of these parties have somehow, for different reasons, become conjoined. And as Myrtle Meades and mothers have small children in common, and as there's not a bat's chance of anything resembling a traditional gymkhana ever taking place here or anywhere else in the locale, an agreeable consensus has been achieved whereby the small children of Cabannes will demonstrate the art of equestrian paneurythmic dancing. Never let it be said that Provence stands still: this is truly avante garde. But, because animals are involved, we need a vet and the other person present in our tableau is no lesser being than a professionally observant Monsieur Villiers. No surprise then that emergency telephones in deep pockets aren't buzzing; no wonder that Madame Martin is concentrating on spice infused saucepans: that ménage á trois interloper is only a matter of metres away. Reader, just when you thought that everything had reached summertime equilibrium, that curly haired fellow from Plan d'Orgon raises his tiny head yet again.

Chapter Thirty One

The following day is, of course, Sunday, but few that have graced these pages are attending church. This is not to say that our story is entirely secular because we know that climactic events are programmed to coincide with the Assumption of the Virgin Mary in the middle of August. And, let's be fair, not too many novels make that sort of claim. Madame Lapin, being quite overwhelmed with civic and political responsibilities, whilst simultaneously trying to juggle a regular presence at the bureau des affaires, and a more than passing contribution to the continuous expansion of the pickle business has little time for love. Something has to give and what has been given, at least temporarily, is Jean-Pierre Lucard.

The paella purveyor is not, unsurprisingly, too worried. To be fair, he was always going to share his onions far and wide. In particular, since he passed that evening at La Plancha, next to the heavily and expensively scented wife of Cheesy Chips O'Connor, Jean-Pierre has pointed his ambitious medallion away from the host nation and trampled onto the lives and wives of the ex-pats. Nonetheless, he is sufficiently astute to recognise that, if you play your ingredients perfectly, you can have your paella and eat it. More to the point, cosmopolitan though he may be in his amorous intentions, Jean-Pierre doesn't want to lose the cricket match commission. Either of them. Consequently, he is one of several in attendance chez Martin where parts of a garlic-clad spring lamb, marinated overnight in red wine with a profusion of herbs in which wild thyme reigns supreme, are now sitting in a slow oven waiting to fall away from the various bones that once held this sheep together.

The tiniest of newish potatoes, and not the Cornish Earlies, have been cooked, doused in olive oil and black pepper and are ready to be the prime accompaniment. And the first of the haricot beans, covered in grated lemon rind and a teasing of crushed garlic comprise the traditional entrée. A well-cooked meal is an essential prerequisite of discussions surrounding the various refreshments that will coincide with cricket matches and paneurythmic gymkhanas; not to mention before and after candlelit processions at the Frigolet Abbey. Horses might fall, balls may be lost and illuminations may fail to ignite, but folk need feeding to a level commensurate with both religious and secular entertainments and festivals.

Apart from the Martins and the paella purveyor, other people present around that trusty table include Madame Lapin, plus Richard and Myrtle Meades. Thus all the ingredients of the refreshment committee are in situ, as are all the necessary components of a potentially fractious forum. Of course, Richard Meades has no immediate need to be at the bottom of the lane having no culinary contribution to offer. In fact, Myrtle's husband would much rather be taking his Sunday lunch elsewhere. For example, the rest of the ex-pat cricket team are, at this very moment, enjoying the barbequed hospitality of Mas Saint Antoine where Ruud is leading the batting over hot coals. Well, gas actually but it doesn't have quite the evocative air of smoke blinding fuel.

Nonetheless, there's rhyme and reason to Richard Meades' presence chez Martin: someone with little desire to be at that particular table is just the sort of person needed to make executive notes and construct a list of sorts in a residence where lists seldom make an appearance. There are so many folk with vested interests in a range of coinciding events at the bottom of the lane that it needs a person of stamina to record and organise competing priorities which can then be aligned to the practical business taking place along the road that runs between Noves and Cabannes. Accordingly, Myrtle's husband has presented an agenda.

It's tricky for a number of reasons. Firstly, the only agenda that most of the others are interested in comprises the order of aperitifs, the arrival of the lamb and the distribution of accompanying wine. Secondly, there are personal but specific priorities to overcome. For example, and in no particular order, there's a small matter of who will provide the cricket tea: the two bonnes madames assume this is their remit but Myrtle Meades, being English, knows more about scones and cucumber sandwiches. Even if that dilemma can be resolved, Jean-Pierre Lucard is of the view that he has only graced this event owing to the fact that he alone is capable of providing all the nutrition anyone can need. And Madame Lapin, already fighting one corner, is, believe it or not, still anxious not to tread on the paella purveyor's sandaled toes.

Further, Monsieur Martin, who has few culinary interests, wants to know the order of events in this over-crowded weekend: specifically, when does the gymkhana occur in relation to the cricket match and when does either of these events take place around the illuminated service to celebrate the Assumption of the Virgin Mary? And his contribution sparks another discussion concerning whether to eat before or after the service at Frigolet and what that meal might comprise. It's little wonder that, at every turn, more wine is called for and more pencils are sharpened.

Reader, be assured that we are not about to take the path of hungry observers along the path of this never-relaxing meal. The participants, regardless of nationality, do their very best to pursue a normal French lunch: which is to say, they try to enjoy superb country food and pleasant conversation at a pace appropriate to arriving at a state of play in which at least some issues have been resolved; even if the score remains unknown.

Chapter Thirty Two

On this particular Sunday, certain patrons of the PMU bar in Cabannes, who would normally be relaxing in that unquestionably salubrious venue, have upped sticks and travelled to a rendezvous at the Bar-Tabac des Alpilles in St Remy. That they successfully managed this feat was quite an accomplishment and not one that was executed without threats, bribery and a considerable amount of moaning on the part of the visitors. Generally, it might have made more sense if the outing was reversed and the French cricket team had met in Cabannes. Usually, the Bar-Tabac des Alpilles in St Remy would have been busy enjoying the fat wallets of the pre-roast, ex-pat contingent. This week, however, most of the male members of the Yorkshire pudding brigade are over at Mas Saint Antoine or at the end of a dusty lane. Thus, given that the Bar-Tabac is a bigger venue with more inviting food than what might be on offer in Cabannes, the French strategic planning meeting is, strategically, being held in St Remy where daube is on the menu. Again.

As with current situations along the road that runs between Noves and Cabannes there is, fortunately, little in the detail of the St Remy summit that needs worry us, dear reader. It's interesting to note that, in this relatively tiny geographical area, men, and some women of importance, are meeting simultaneously to hold similarly themed discussions. If we were inclined towards some notion of critical analysis, we might conclude that the general aim of all three meetings is to decide who is standing where and doing what in which order on what day. Alternatively, if we were interested in a symbiotic conclusion, which is doubtful, especially after the aperitif, we might wonder how the discussions in all three meetings can ever coincide to form the basis of a subsequent weekend's celebrations. And if we were the type of folk fascinated only by the voyeuristic nitty gritty of other people's lives, we might wonder why Monsieur Villiers is at the Bar-Tabac des Alpilles and where he's going next. Oh wait – that's us then.

In the logical world, Monsieur Villiers, being a veterinary practitioner with an interest in small spotted ponies, might be expected to be present at the meeting being held at the bottom of a dusty lane. However, as Monsieur Villiers is also a veterinary practitioner with an interest in small married pickle purveyors, that venue is a non-starter. Monsieur Villiers, although once deemed an intruder from Marseilles, and latterly resident in a place where none but the hardiest hero hunters venture, is, nonetheless a Provençale. Thus, he is neither an ex-pat nor a man who is inclined to play cricket for the other side (unless you consider someone else's wife to constitute 'the other side'). Moreover, there's no getting away from the fact that he's going to be present in some sort of professional capacity at the quasi-religious sporting weekend, so he has to be somewhere. And as the French have an, albeit minor, interest in the outcome of the gymkhana, and no interest whatsoever in who's doing what with someone else's wife, as long as it's not their wife, the vet's presence in St Remy is without question.

To be fair, Monsieur Villiers is more than a little bored with it all. He's not the only one: down at the bottom of a lane that runs from you know where, Madame Martin is heartily sick of people and their plans. Don't think she's altogether abandoned Provençal expectations. Hours have been spent with that dead sheep: herbs have been gathered and tenderly and tenderisingly massaged into its young and pliant skin. Tiny cuts have been made into which crushes of thyme and slivers of garlic have been slotted. Wine, olive oil and carefully cut accompaniments have been prepared; plates have been warmed and filled and the well-being of the immediate world is subject exclusively to her professional, but tiny, nuances.

None of this will matter to Madame Martin once the meal is served. Her role of the day will have been successfully accomplished. And because she's one of this world's organisers, all the necessary preparation for the forthcoming week will also be in place. There's nothing like a spot of practical and psychological groundwork to allow room for oneself. She knows that everyone present will be too full of sheep and wine and plans to worry about who's clearing the table afterwards. Or where the chef is.

Likewise, Monsieur Villiers has a number of things in hand over at St Remy. For a start, he has all sorts of useful information regarding the French position on almost anything apart from the positions in a French cricket team. And all sorts of other people might be interested in what he knows, although he doubts it. The important thing is that he's participated: he's an accessory with a small foot in a number of camps which is always potentially useful, even if that undefinable notion of home is preferable. More importantly at the moment is that, like Madame Martin, he's performed some sort of unspoken but useful role of which no-one is aware.

Consequently, both parties are able to make discrete departures from their respective venues without, it seems, anyone raising an alcohol infused eyelid. Reader, this in itself is a paradoxical sadness and one that does not bode well for happy endings. Our two protagonists have fumbled their sorry way through these pages of hitherto happiness. Now, Madame Martin has more to lose in respect of our dear Henri with his small spotted ponies. We want happy endings shared under the setting of the Provençal sun. We have no desire for real life.

Having met at the point on the road between Noves and Cabannes where Madame Martin unexpectedly saw the coypu, these two make their way in that battered red car up into La Montagnette and onto the meadows of Frigolet that they love so much. The Sunday masses are over until the evening and they wander amongst the cicada humming grasses where a few families are enjoying a late-in-the-day picnic. Latterly, Monsieur Villiers has been reading Mistral's memoirs and tells Madame Martin about the largely unknown school that was once situated here. However, Monsieur Villiers has also been reading more up-to-date water-based information written not on ancient leaves by the laureate, but on the harsh-to-the-eyes pages sur l'internet.

Somehow, despite the tribulations of cookery and cricket that have been somewhat drenched in aperitifs and accompaniments, the two escapees manage to climb to a point above Frigolet where they can look upon the southern reaches of Provence. They've been here before, of course, but this afternoon the day is still clear enough to view the distant sparkling sea. And water is always inviting. Madame Martin would like nothing better than to journey down through the Camargue to the place where the salt water laps against the shore at Saint Mairies de la Mer. Given half the chance, Madame Martin would gladly throw herself into the Mediterranean and swim in the opposite direction to those latter day migrants from the Holy Land. For the time being, she keeps this thought to herself.

Monsieur Villiers, meanwhile, is thinking of longer and narrower water courses. He recently read a novel about a man who brought a waterborne bookshop from Paris to Avignon. The vet has been greatly inspired and recounts the story to his companion. Madame Martin who, unable to recall the last time she actually read a book is, nonetheless, quite taken with the general theme which, naturally, has nothing to do with her own small life. The idea of living on a boat on the Rhône, meeting all sorts of interesting folk, or simply hiding away, is endearing. And she makes the mistake of telling the vet this.

'All things are possible', says Monsieur Martin enigmatically. 'And it doesn't have to be the Rhône. What about the Canal du Midi?'

'Canal or river', she responds, 'what does that have to do with me? That job's done and the story is written. And anyway, I don't have any books', she continues.

'Bien sûr', an enthusiastic small curly haired man replies. 'But you have pickles. And jam. And a reputation'.

The cicadas momentarily cease their chattering. The brown butterflies with the frayed wings halt their fluttering. The hitherto indiscernible breeze that has worried the grasses becomes conspicuous by its sudden absence. And somewhere on a distant peak of the Alpilles, Bonelli's unseen eagle drops silently on its prey. And in this small moment in time, Madame Martin sees her brave new world which encompasses all that she might have visualised had she ever allowed herself the glory of imagination.

'We don't have a boat,' she says in a very tiny voice.

Chapter Thirty Three

Suddenly, the second week in August has arrived once more and events that were born in last November's mistral are heading towards a conclusion. All that pillar to post nonsense chez Shaker is about to reach fruition. That meeting of the tall and the short by the fence where diseased pear trees once stood will imminently transpose into a possible equine assault on the senses. And all of our protagonists, major and minor, will reap a harvest of sorts. The scenes are well and truly set.

Act One

It's been a long time since so many people have turned down the dusty lane that runs from the road between Noves and Cabannes. In fact, it's unlikely that such a crowd have ever previously undertaken this route, at least not all at the same time. To aid those who might not be quite certain where to leave the road, Phyllida rises at une bonne heure with a tin of white paint and a large brush. Helpfully, she's painted a series of large circles around the telegraph pole at the end of the lane. Consequently, the road is scarred with tell-tale skid marks: cars, trucks and scooters that came round the bend in full French throttle are scattered amongst the bamboo that shades this infamous junction. Stalking Norwegian Blues who had been enjoying a quiet morning impersonating closely related cousins of the Serengeti have long since fled this unexpected safari. Conversely, Clovis and Gabriel are in their element with all these ankles at which to offer a random welcoming snap.

The partner who cannot be named might also be expected to be in hiding somewhere or other as the hordes pass by. However, he is busy with chairs, but not of the variety to be found in a Swedish catalogue. In fact, every spare chair in the vicinity, with the notable exception of the body clinching chaise longue, currently forms part of a huge wooden and plastic circle around the edge of the paddock chez Martin. Amongst this new theatrical arena, bales of straw also make a not infrequent appearance. And even if folk still find themselves without a ready-made seat – no problem: blankets and coverlets that have been passed down the generations who draped them over ancient beds and sofas have, today, found a new anticipatory role.

To the rear chez Martin, close to a once overgrown path that led to a previously cage-ensconced wolf-dog, an informal bar has been established. Councillor Lapin, having obtained bureaucratic permission from the commune, is directly responsible for this coup which has, it must be said, angered the proprietor of the PMU bar in Cabannes. Still, the two bonnes madames are more than able to cope with internecine disagreements. In any case, they are supplementing their most recent invention of peach wine with a supply of the red stuff curtesy of the PMU bar and have managed to persuade Christophe and Michel to attend to the visitors' liquid needs. And to the left of this refreshment stand, Jean-Pierre Lucard has set up his paella stall. As we speak, the combined waft of Camarguaise rice, sea-food and a hearty helping of onions is drifting down wind. Well, on this mistral-free day, there isn't actually any wind but you know what I mean.

And finally, it's time for the gymkhana. On hearing Monsieur Martin make this announcement, the wine-supping, baguette munching crowd are somewhat surprised. An agenda had been previously drawn up and distributed but, this being deeply rural Provence, no-one had actually expected the timings to be adhered to. They've arrived on the correct date and it's only an hour later than proceedings were supposed to proceed so folk are anticipating further opportunity for catching up on local news. Moreover, there's no sign of any jumps having been erected in the paddock; just an old wooden table behind which the latter-day seat distributor now stands. Monsieur Martin must be getting confused in his dotage they think and resume their good natured gossiping, drinking and munching.

But the partner who cannot be named has quit the chair business in order to assume his role as musical director. He is now in charge of a ghetto blaster: an item so ancient that it may well comprise an archaeological discovery. As the initial notes of Beinsa Douno reverberate gently around the paddock, the crowd fall silent. What is this? Hardly La Marseillaise or any other music appropriately stirring for competitive events. Not even all that jazz of which so many rumours have floated across the air waves of the past. On the other hand, there's something attention grabbing in a kind of strangely soporific way about this new type of music. Should anyone have a camera to hand, the ensuing snap will surely cause consternation to someone who finds a battered and torn copy stuck between the leaves of a very old tome in the distant future. What, they will ask, can have caused that group of rural types relaxing in a summer field to have paused, half empty glasses trapped forever in the no man's land between neck and mouth? Why do teeth remain for all time sunk into never-to-be-finished baguettes? Why do all those many and varied eyes share that sense of unexplained amazement?

For into their circle of life glides a tall and ghostly apparition: a woman draped all in white: an ankle length skirt, a baggy cheesecloth shirt, possibly of even older provenance than the ghetto blaster, a shawl thrown carelessly around her shoulders and a wide-brimmed hat with a floating veil that, in truth, wouldn't look out of place in a bee-keeper's wardrobe. One of the two madames, who have temporarily abandoned domestic duties in order to watch the so-called gymkhana, has joined the ranks of the speechless. Madame Martin is silently wondering how her husband, who is currently absent, can have allowed this ridiculous giant to invade his miniature riding school. Conversely, Councillor Lapin, also stunned into silence by Myrtle Meades, who is now gracefully dancing alone around the paddock to the sounds of Beinsa Douno, holds, it must be said, even more silent admiration for Myrtle's outfit. 'Could be considered quite romantic', she admits to herself. 'On a person of proper proportions', she adds to no-one.

Wondering why the demand for drinks and paella has dried up, Christophe, Michel and Jean-Pierre Lucard make their way to the perimeter of the paddock. Reader, it's quite pointless for your narrator to record their ensuing comments: this is not a story that entertains obscenities. Jean-Pierre Lucard is horrified to notice what can only be described as admiration on the face of his sometimes-lover. Putain. Needless to say, those three musketeers turn tail in the direction of glasses of the red stuff. Could be a long day. Thus, they miss the entrance of the little children of Cabannes, also dressed engagingly from head to toe in white, and not a riding hat between them. Beinsa Douno, encouraged by the musical director, raises the volume as Myrtle Meades turns to greet her prodigies and lead them in dance on a further tour of the paddock. The obliging parents, who have now, thankfully, returned to eating and drinking and suchlike, cheer with relief (even if they're wondering where the ponies might be).

The children of Cabannes perform a wondrous dance with much swaying of arms and bowing of tiny bodies. The grown-ups of Cabannes have never before seen such a spectacle and are entranced by their offspring (even if they're still wondering where the ponies might be. Those would be the ponies they've paid for their children to have lessons with). Don't despair reader: before patience can be exhausted, before mumblings and grumblings can commence, before moaning and groaning takes centre stage, Myrtle Meades guides the little equestrians back to the make-shift entrance of the even more make-shift arena where, at last, Monsieur Martin is waiting with the small spotted ponies. As Beinsa Douno achieves another climax, Myrtle Meades, Monsieur Martin, the children of Cabannes, Hebdo, Georges, Cabut and all the other ponies make their grand entrance. Never before in the long and unknown history of paneurthymy have ponies danced with such meaning.

Fetlocks lift with sublime synchronicity and hooves are held high as manes are tossed aside with musical abandon. Heads back, the little white riders now aboard their mounts, lift one arm, then the other like a host of angelic cherubs offering salutation to the glory of the Provençal sunshine. The audience, having overcome their temporary catatonic state, tip back their glasses and reach for grown-up sized refills. Momentarily discarded baguettes are once more bitten into with fervour as Beinsa Douno, aided by peach wine and the rosé of the Ventoux, instigates the onset of almost group hysteria. Some of the men trot back to the makeshift bar with a view to moving to the red stuff and others hurry to place provisional paella orders with Jean-Pierre Lucard.

Back in the ring, meanwhile, under his protective but uniform straw hat, Monsieur Martin wears the biggest smile that we have witnessed in all of these pages and others. As Myrtle Meades dances in and out of the actors, Monsieur Martin guides the ponies into a circle in readiness for the finale. When all of the audience members have retaken their various seats and replenished all their many and diverse drinking vessels, Myrtle Meades gives an unseen signal upon which the children of Cabannes dismount and stand quietly by the beautiful heads of the small spotted ponies. The partner who cannot be named silences Beinsa Douno and a hush falls over the arena like a giant horse blanket. It is a hush so loud that, once more, the paella purveyor, the three musketeers and the two bonnes madames are drawn away from their respective enterprises in order to see what has happened. With everyone in place, the hand of the partner who cannot be named performs a deft movement on the ghetto blaster and the unmistakable opening notes of La Marseillaise ring out. Those that are seated join those who are standing and the cicadas are silenced by a tumultuous rendition of the national anthem.

Act Two

And afterwards, all silences having been silenced, and all suspicions suffocated in a sea of emotion, there is much cheering and effusive kissing of anyone and everyone including, most of all, that unlikely heroine, Myrtle Meades. Children are being cherished, ponies are being petted and Monsieur Martin is king for a day. A picnic fit for the annals of history begins in earnest and will continue well into the evening when Jean-Pierre Lucard, having sold out of everything, packs up his stall and heads back to Orange to make tomorrow's batch of paella in readiness for the cricket match. But while all of this is taking place, a phone vibrates in an old apron pocket and Phyllida, who has been somewhat of a bystander in today's activities, notices Madame Martin sidling into the brambles with a tiny hand to her almost invisible ear. Amongst all the bonhomie, well-being and, let's face it, general drunkenness, Phyllida experiences an inexplicable degree of anxiety.

Chapter Thirty Four

That evening, the air in Cabannes is merry with diverse celebrations. In the homes of the parents of paneurythmic children, celebratory dinners are enjoyed with all of the extended kith and kin who were present at the gymkhana plus those who see no reason for missing an unexpected feast even if they'd been unable or unwilling to pass the preceding hours of daylight on ground where diseased pear trees had once stood.

Meanwhile, in the PMU bar, those members of the French cricket team who will seek glory tomorrow are partaking of pre-celebratory practise refreshment. In this, they are enthusiastically encouraged by supporters and a number of folk who have assumed the mantle of team physiotherapist, team psychologist, team medic, team coach and any other necessary adjutants as the fancy takes hold. And those men whose positions overlap the two camps – that is those who are paneurythmic parents AND cricketers or team officials – pass half the evening indoors on instructions of their recently enfranchised and empowered wives, and the rest of the time in the bar with the men whose wives are only too pleased to be ridding their homes of such irritations for an evening.

A not entirely dissimilar group of men, differentiated only by language, are currently in situ at Charlie O'Connor's place, Mas Saint Antoine being unavailable due to guests. This is, of course, the ex-pat team and a few extras who are receiving last minute instruction on the game plan from Jack Shaker. Buddy, bored with this interminable nonsense that seems to have been going on for months, if not years in doggy terms, has curled himself into a sulky furry ball in front of the place where a fire might be roaring were this December. Three or four opened bottles of the red stuff decorate the sitting room but Team Ex-Pat members are relatively fastidious in comparison with the PMU congregation. Jack Shaker is resolved that moderation is key this evening. Thus, we have accounted for quite a number of those who have graced these pages at some point. But what about the whereabouts of the main protagonists?

Jean-Pierre Lucard remains in Orange to whence he bid a hasty retreat once the equine events were done with. Reader, you might find this surprising given that there are groups of men about with whom he could enthusiastically engage. But think on: as part of today's various successes, all of his paneurythmic paella was consumed. Tomorrow's cricket match looks even more promising so Jean-Pierre is more than happy to hide his shiny medallion behind a freshly laundered chef's apron and forfeit an evening in the company of other real men.

Councillor Lapin, meanwhile, has little spare time to consider whether she's been by-passed in favour of drinking companions or another batch of paella as she, too, is an active member of yet another group that has formed this evening. The avant-garde kitchen of Mas Saint Antoine, being currently out of bounds due to the presence of seasonal guests, Christine has driven the two bonnes madames and Phyllida, along with hampers of ingredients, into Noves; specifically, to the not-so-avant-garde but more-than-adequate kitchen of Myrtle Meades. Having previously undertaken instruction from Myrtle on the intricacies of cricket lunches and cricket teas, the four cooks are now honing their culinary skills to cosmopolitan perfection. Tomorrow's repasts will be like no other seen in these parts.

Ruud has stayed at Mas Saint Antoine in case any guests have pressing needs and Christophe, obviously, is with friends and cricketing colleagues in Cabannes. So that just leaves Monsieur Martin and the partner who cannot be named. And, of course, Clovis and Gabriel. The latter pair in this quartet is taking advantage of the peace and quiet of the kitchen floor chez Martin. Given an invitation, they would've been more than happy to accompany Monsieur Martin to the other side of the fence that divides the land where diseased pear trees once stood. These days, however, they are personae non gratae. Gabriel possesses none of that caution that his father displays in the face of Norwegian Blues. The young upstart, conversely, delights in encouraging the old man in a spot of cat baiting and the pair are, therefore, no longer placed in a position to outstay a welcome.

This evening, the aperitif is taken on the dog-free terrace. Monsieur Martin has no desire to do anything that might upset his dear friend. No spring chickens, these two are tired but happy in each other's company and that of a few musical Bulgarians. As a special treat, the partner who cannot be named has opened a chilled bottle of his very special Sancerre. The cicadas have closed down their noisy shutters for the day and the first of tonight's owls journeys cross the paddock to rest on a favourite branch of one of the lime trees that line the road that runs between Noves and Cabannes.

Monsieur Martin is delighted that the gymkhana went so well and even more thrilled that he has no planned involvement in tomorrow's proceedings. Well, not until the evening when he will take Madame Martin up to La Montagnette for the service to celebrate the Assumption of the Virgin Mary at Frigolet. Thus far, Monsieur Martin is the unsung hero of these two celebratory days: it was surely a magnificent expression of insight to plan the more than secular events to coincide with traditional religiosity. In the meantime, he and the partner have worked together quietly and methodically putting away chairs, replacing straw bales in more suitable environments and generally tidying up the paddock prior to settling the small spotted ponies down for the night.

But just as the two friends are silently reflecting on the excellent good fortune bestowed upon them by the very nature of where they live, a motorcycle screeches noisily into the lane. With the engine still running, the machine is thrown into the dust and Christophe bursts through the gate in a state of extreme agitation.

'Merde', thinks Monsieur Martin, 'now what?'

'Putain', thinks the partner who cannot be named as he secretes his half full, only-for-special-people bottle of Sancerre under the table.

'Papa', shouts Christophe, 'that idiot Mesquin has issued a ban on all people associated with cricket entering the arena tomorrow'. And to cut a long story to the quick, it transpires that the only way of going ahead with the cricket match is to hold it in the field on the opposite side of the lane to where diseased pear trees once stood. It's too late to do anything this evening other than relay messages and calls for help to various members of diverse groups in their respective meetings.

It's an unexpected end to this momentous day, but one that causes little disturbance to the old timers. Thus, dear reader, as we await the morning with some trepidation, everyone is accounted for. Apart from the vet from Plan d'Orgon.

Chapter Thirty Five

Act One

To say this morning commences at une bonne heure doesn't really convey the whole truth of the matter. In reality, the dawning of this day is more akin to those in certain other French enterprises; notably those involving a still, where business must be concluded before certain officials from the EU leave their beds. Given the various types of preparation undertaken last night by diverse cricket-related groups, the presence of so many people, of all nationalities, along the lane before the sun has even dared to show its face, only vindicates the importance of today's match. Teams and allegiances are temporarily abandoned as the French and the ex-pats work together to hastily prepare a last minute cricket pitch in the field we rarely mention.

Monsieur Martin moves the small spotted ponies into the safety of the paddock for the day and the partner who cannot be named once again strikes up his role in the seating business. This cannot be accomplished alone as today each of those engaged in undermining the edict of Mayor Mesquin has been requested to bring at least one chair with them. The gymkhana was well attended but todays expected audience is far greater. Meanwhile, Christophe, who has never before been observed at such an early hour, unless he was arriving home from somewhere or other, is busily engaged in the carpentry department. Christophe has not received much in the way of good press in these pages. Generally, he has appeared located at a point somewhere between indolent and comatose. However, he has shown surprising, if sporadic, stages of action regards the community and now we find him, hammer and nails to hand, knocking up a necessary score board from bits of old wood that litter chez Martin. Displaying the number of runs is paramount when the French destroy the ex-pats.

Sadly, there's no time to construct a pavilion and Madame Martin is adamant that her home will not be invaded by teams of any nationality. No matter. The weather bodes well, as it always does, and teams can easily congregate outdoors. And speaking of that good lady, she and her sous chefs are quite relieved not to have to transport assorted components of English cricket-type cuisine down to the arena in Cabannes. Life, for them, has suddenly become oh-so-much easier even if confidence levels are low respecting egg and cress. Madame Lapin, who is clothed in vaguely paneurythmic vogue á la Meades (although she would never admit to her source of inspiration), is concerned about Madame Martin's demeanour. To all intents and purposes, Madame Martin appears pragmatic in her early morning culinary duties but something is not quite right.

'Seems a little distracted n'est-ce pas?', suggests the enigmatically dressed Madame Lapin to Phyllida.

'Something's wrong', agrees the lady from the other side of the fence. Phyllida is the very essence of discretion but is troubled to learn that she's not alone in identifying something worrying. 'I saw her in the brambles on the phone yesterday'.

'What phone?' demands the councillor. 'What do you mean, in the brambles?'

But before the conversation can proceed, Madame Martin approaches with a number of hard boiled eggs to hand. 'Are these chopped or mashed?' she enquires. And the moment is lost as just then, Jean-Pierre Lucard arrives looking somewhat less than his normal cool self.

'Putain! Why didn't you tell me?' In all the forward and backward communications of the previous evening, precipitated by Monsieur Mesquin's late-in-the day decision to forbid use of the arena for cricket-type activities, no-one had informed the paella purveyor that paella was not to be purveyed in Cabannes. Everyone had thought that someone else would relay the news to Orange. In the event, no-one had and Jean-Pierre's view of himself as the most important man on the planet has been somewhat diminished. His golden medallion is hanging limply and his bronzed face is spotted with beads of sweat. Madame Lapin looks at her sometimes lover and is rather horrified by this emergence of true nature. Jean-Pierre Lucard happens to spot this look of disdain but, having never seen such a look before fails to recognise it. 'Merde', he thinks, 'what's she wearing? Looks like a phantom'.

Act Two

Once more, the crowds head down the lane that saunters from the road running between Noves and Cabannes. Today, however, there are far more visitors than those that turned out for the paneurythmic gymkhana. For the cricket match has taken on the mantle of national pride. Accordingly, families from both Noves and Cabannes, along with ex-pats from a wider environment, are already competing for position in the make-shift audience enclosure within the field generally inhabited by small spotted ponies. Amongst all the late-in-the-day or early-in-the-morning planning, no-one has considered the possibility of dividing the area into sections depending on nationality. No matter: the spectators manage to find their ways into respective divisions with little trouble.

Christophe and Michel, being integral to the well-being of the French team's performance, are unable to man the bar. To be truthful, Christophe, Michel and indeed the majority of the French team members look, this morning, as if they will be unable to man very much. The previous evening's pre-celebratory drinks have taken an apparent toll. Conversely, the ex-pat team, who, under the wise tutelage of Jack Shaker, practised considerably more refined moderation, appear smugly confident. Monsieur le patron from the Bar-Tabac des Alpilles has volunteered his services to run the liquid refreshment stall this morning. He, too, has observed the difference in team presentation and decides to embark on a spot of multicultural bonhomie, possibly with an ulterior motive.

'Monsieur', he approaches Jack Shaker. 'Why not commence the proceedings in a good-humoured, non-partisan mode', he suggests.

'What do you mean?' the ex-pat team manager responds suspiciously.

'Bring your men over to have a pre-match aperitif with the opposition'.

'But it's only half past nine', Jack points out. Buddy offers a duty driven supportive snarl although secretly hopes croissants might be involved in the proceedings. Monsieur le patron is confused by Jack's reference to time and looks to Ruud who has also taken over part-time bar duties in order to balance things up.

'Not a bad idea', says Ruud. 'Could get messy otherwise. Gives a good example to the spectators'. All three turn to look at the crowds who have already begun squabbling amongst the hay bales and eclectic selection of seating arrangements. Thus, Jack Shaker brings his energised team over to the make-do bar with instructions to engage in a little geniality. The ex-pats are wary and flex their team muscles in what they think is a threatening sort of way.

'Can't hurt', advises Cheesy Chips O'Connor. 'A small rosé is harmless; barely noticeable,' and he calls his colleagues to order.

'Too early for rosé', remarks Monsieur le patron. 'We drink Pastis for breakfast'. The now congregated ex-pats are a little taken aback but, nonetheless, decide it wouldn't be cricket to refuse. Unseen by most present, Christophe tips the wink to Monsieur le patron and plastic tumblers are duly filled. And, naturally, the first harmless glass, curtesy of the French, needs to be followed by another paid for by the ex-pats. Don't worry reader. It doesn't get too out of hand although the first two rounds have to be symmetrically positioned against another two before the teams can stagger off to their respective muster points.

Somewhere along the line, a coin is thrown into the warm Provençal air and Team Ex-Pat find themselves batting for the morning. The partner who cannot be named is, against his better judgement, appointed as an umpire on the grounds of impartiality. Subsequently, he is currently positioned behind the stumps, unhappily dressed in an assorted range of discarded clothing.

'We need another umpire at square leg', the partner points out. The French are confused by this statement which is lost in translation. Everyone looks around; largely they are looking for a square leg, although they also want to know who the second umpire is. And just at this moment, when doors and knocking do not comprise a feasible entrance, a small red car bumps its way along the dusty lane and comes to a sudden halt near the front door chez Martin.

'Putain', thinks a bystander who goes under the name of Monsieur Martin. 'What's he doing here?'

'Just the man', says Monsieur le patron, and before Monsieur Villiers can draw breath, he finds himself under the alias of square leg next to Christophe who, although he is unaware, is standing mid-wicket.

Christophe looks down on a mop of black curly hair. 'What's your game?' he asks breathing Pastis laden fumes on the vet. Reader, there can only be one answer. And frankly, do we want to go over this fiasco ball by potentially tedious ball? Possibly. There are discussions and fallings out but the ex-pats believe they have the upper hand: they know about cricket. It's important to understand that, in this friendly match, the word 'friendly' is immediately discarded once Michel, positioned at short leg, retires after the first ball, lobbed by Harry Larwood, causes a temporary concussion necessitating first aid at the bar. The umpire who cannot be named begins to make himself unusually unpopular given his general geniality; the problem being, he knows more cricket rules than anyone else imagines ever existed. Harry Larwood, upon whom various fielders descend in order to avenge their wounded colleague, crawls out from under the scrum and demands a call of obstruction.

'No obstruction', announces the umpire who cannot be named. 'You are not in the process of attempting to hit the ball'.

'Sledging', shouts the second umpire and everyone on the field turns to the man from Plan d'Orgon with a view to mass abuse.

'Group obstruction', demands Cheesy Chips O'Connor from the other end. 'All fielders to be removed from the pitch'. Immediately, those enjoying the attack on the second umpire turn to vent their anger on Charlie and the match is in danger of being called to a halt before it has barely begun. A shrill, high-pitched whine calls the players to sudden order: the umpire who cannot be named is in possession of a secret whistle. Just the job it seems until a further interruption ensues.

Clovis, who has been watching events from the boundary with his son, does not like whistles. In fact, Clovis has never heard a whistle before but, now that he has, he definitely knows that they are an instrument of torture. Worse still, Gabriel is crying. Clovis, in all his previously known-but-thought-lost snarling glory, runs onto the pitch with Gabriel in close pursuit. The spectators rise as one and cheer on the dogs. They had no idea that this ridiculous game could be so entertaining. Men of all races scatter in the face of the almost-a-pack of angry canines but Clovis has only one man in his sights. He leaps at the appalled partner, knocks the whistle out of the offending mouth, delicately picks it up with his wolf like teeth and runs off. Gabriel, in awe of his father, follows him back chez Martin, taking the cricket ball along for good measure.

Everyone on the pitch, including the rest of the batsmen who arrive like a disordered cavalry to support their team members, suddenly remember that they are grown men and begin to check the well-being of both teams and umpires. There is a lot of hand-shaking and some kissing on the part of the French. The two umpires partake of a little conversation and, having ensured that order has been fully restored, the one that cannot be named makes his call:

'Twelfth man'. Once this decree has been explained to the French fielders they are ecstatic until they realise that, not previously knowing about the twelfth man rule, their team is not in possession of anyone who comes at any point after number eleven. Captain Jack has a suggestion:

'Why not bring on Jean-Pierre Lucard?'

Henri is dismissive: 'Good idea', he accedes, 'but no good for the afternoon. He'll be replenishing his paella.'

'Doesn't matter,' explains Captain Jack, 'he won't be allowed to bat'. The French fielders look as if things are about to turn nasty again.

'What do you mean, he can't bat,' they demand? The whistleless umpire explains that the substitute can only field; another rule that the fielders find devoid of any obvious logic. Still, it does provide an immediate solution to the diminished team. Someone goes off to break the news to the man from Orange and Myrtle Meades, sensing an opportune moment, arrives on the pitch with quarters of different types of orange. Yet again, the French are mystified but resign themselves to this unexpected refreshment. There are mutterings and grumblings but, suddenly, a cheer goes up from the spectators as, chef's apron discarded in favour of the preferred unbuttoned look, the paella purveyor strides into glory. The umpire without a whistle thinks about mentioning dress code but thinks again. Monsieur Villiers arrives at the same time with the rediscovered ball and the match finally proceeds.

Men stagger in and men fall out. The umpires call a halt for lunch at noon at which point the ex-pats have scored eighty-six for eight. And this being a one-day game, they are forced to declare, upon which declaration both teams make their way to the lunch table.

Act Three

Cricket is hardly cricket without a pavilion but who needs one of the traditional construct in the height of August? The teams repair to long trestle tables under the bat yielding willows on which have been placed jugs of ice-cold water and carafes of rosé supplied by Monsieur Martin and the heroic owners of the PMU bar in Cabannes and the Bar-Tabac des Alpilles in St Remy respectively. The two bonnes madames have prepared baguettes stuffed with merguez sausage and an assortment of pickles which act sufficiently as a handy means of soaking up the liquid refreshment. Madame Lapin, having temporarily regained an interest in her occasional paramour, glides round Jean-Pierre Lucard entranced by his newly discovered sporting prowess. In truth, the paella purveyor's diverse prowess was never really uncovered but Madame Lapin is undeterred. Twelfth man has a ring of the courts about it and he has therefore gone up and off on a new tangent as far as she's concerned. The twelfth man, however, is now an important team member and only has time for his compatriots as they discuss strategy and tactics. Other interested parties at this feast have more than two short legs between them as Clovis, Gabriel and Buddy form a snarling menagerie of food collectors under the tables.

Lunch is a reasonably brief affair given the potential to copiously imbibe that pink wine which feels so insignificant on a summer's day. Jack Shaker is strict with his team and Christophe, observing this, tries to instil similar willpower in the French. In fact, the French team have learned a lot this morning and are surprisingly keen to resume the match and with it, their innings. This keenness comes as a surprise to the spectators, some of whom, having missed their weekly stake at the PMU bar, are currently taking bets on the afternoon's outcome. Let's face it, eighty six runs is not an enormous score; must be easy for the French team to beat this they think.

The partner who cannot be named, and who would like to run away to the comfort of his Bulgarian enhanced terrace on any side of a fence that doesn't involve bats, balls and rules, announces the commencement of the afternoon's continuation. The ex-pat team disperse themselves accordingly in diversely named positions whilst Gaston and Michel turn to the wickets. It's a gentle start to the afternoon's activities and, cheered on by the rest of their team, these two speedily notch up ten runs. Captain Jack and his somewhat sluggish team suddenly realise that they could be easily thrashed and up their game.

Richard 'the giant' Meades takes a long run and bowls a straight ball at Michel. The ferocity of this delivery momentarily stuns the spectators. Michel moves forward in order to attain a better position and the ferocious ball lands on a part of the body which may well prevent him from fathering children in the near or far future. As Michel folds in two, the reluctant Monsieur Villiers is concerned that he may now have to apply his veterinary knowledge to the distressed parts of Michel's well-being. However, the umpire who cannot be named has already called leg before wicket. Once again, the teams are embroiled in dispute as Dickie Sparrow claims that Michel has caused an obstruction by stepping forward and extending his manhood.

'Thirteenth man,' asks Gaston hopefully?

Thus it continues until, at a point when the French team has achieved a dangerous score of fifty four for six, the umpires call a halt for tea. Apart from the ex-pats and their supporters, no-one knows quite what this comprises. Players amble off the pitch in the general direction of the trestle tables which have now been clothed in white linen. The make-do, make-shift bar has closed for the afternoon and tea-cups adorn the linen. Tiny triangular sandwiches, filled with crushed egg and cress, are piled onto ancient china plates that Madame Martin recently found in a chest in the shed. Two grand platters support an even grander selection of miniscule gateaux. The ladies stand by anxiously.

'Merde,' says Monsieur Martin and disappears away to check on the small spotted ponies.

'Putain,' growls Christophe, 'what's this?'

And the umpires gird their loins in expectation of further trouble. Some of the spectators snigger and begin to take photographs of the afternoon tea. But the French team members are charmed and these sweaty men shoo away the unwanted audience before delicately helping themselves to their first finger buffet. Graciously, they thank the ladies for the unusual spread. The ex-pat cricketers are unfazed and dive in greedily until they notice the style with which the opposition is taking tea.

'They seem worryingly calm,' observes Charlie O'Connor as he crams three triangles into his mouth.

'Better slow down chaps,' advises Captain Jack. 'They'll think we're panicking.'

'Should we be worried?' asks Harry Larwood.

'It's a blip,' the captain reassures him. 'Beginners' luck. There's only an hour of play left. They'll never score enough in such a short time.' Reader, are these the famous last words that will be written into the annals of local history along with egg and cress sandwiches?

'Nice china,' notes Charlie as he absentmindedly turns over an empty plate to look for the mark of a Swedish catalogue. 'Bloody hell, have you seen this?' But before he can elaborate on his discovery, the umpire who cannot be named calls an end to tea and instructs the teams to return to the field.

There is a veritable buzz amongst the spectators. Even this late in the day, more bets are taken and odds are revised. Some of those in the ex-pat section of the audience who have already placed their euro on a grand-scale win by their team, now sense an upset of historic proportions and secretly hand over more money in a somewhat unpatriotic manner. The book-keeper, otherwise known as the owner of the PMU bar takes account of his accounts and suspends the book. A degree of uproar ensues during which one or two outbreaks of in-fighting might be observed. Largely, though, everyone is more intent on observing play. The scoreboard already accounts for another ten runs.

Billy Botham has had enough of all this sporting bonhomie. He walks away from the stumps to a place that is almost at the end of the lane that runs from the road between Noves and

Cabannes. Just as the French batsmen think he must have gone home, Billy turns and runs at speed towards the crease. During this startling run, his limbs assume all possible permutations but he miscalculates: as the ball leaves Billy's grasp and makes its way to a contact point with the wicket, his arm remains extended with one finger pointing:

'Howzat?' demands Billy as the stumps divide and fall to the ground.

'Howzat?' demand the rest of the ex-pats as they pat each other on the back in a joyous group huddle.

'Comment c'est quoi?' asks Gaston.

'No ball,' states the umpire au fait with the website of the Museum of Rural Life. 'Straight arm'. And yet another heated debate follows. Reader, you were warned that this story would not account for every single ball. Suffice it to say that in the following forty minutes, just about every cricket rule ever invented, plus a few which evolve today, are tested and broken but, for the ex-pat team, all to no avail. At the end of it all, and against the earlier odds, the French team somehow manage to win the day by a margin of three runs. There is uproar. The spectators invade the pitch. A huge fight breaks out round Monsieur le sometime-book-keeper and Jean-Pierre Lucard, donning his apron once more, fires up the hot plates. 'Things are looking good,' he thinks smugly as he reheats the paella.

Chapter Thirty Six

Aperitif

By seven o clock, the trestle tables have been relieved of not-so-white linen and the ancient china, recently beloved by Cheesy Chips O'Connor. Make-do tea-pots have been returned to neighbourly homes from whence they were temporarily donated.

'Won't be using them again,' Madame Martin quietly muses. She's had a long day and it's not over yet. There is nothing to eat in the way of left-overs as the ingredients of afternoon tea were fully consumed by the team members and any detritus was helpfully disposed of by friendly canines. The kitchen chez Martin has returned to an orderly fashion and is ready for anyone to use however they wish the following day. Madame Martin, her sous chefs and neighbours are relieved to have no responsibility for supper, that task being in the wandering hands of Jean-Pierre Lucard.

Many of the players and spectators have retired to their respective abodes for a short rest before the commencement of the paella supper. The hard core, however, remain in situ as Christophe and Gaston have re-opened the make-shift bar. The partner who cannot be named is currently taking a well-earned, mint-infused aperitif on his terrace in the company of a number of Bulgarian musicians and four Norwegian Blues. He has just about regained his equilibrium having vowed to himself never to listen to Beinsa Douno or peruse the website of the Museum of Rural Life at any point during the rest of the days he is granted in Provence. Quietly sitting alongside are Ruud and Monsieur Martin, watching the long day's sky evolve colourfully into evening. Frankly, there's little need of conversation and mostly they are too exhausted to bother.

The women in in their lives, who have little comprehension of how to relax, are busy washing away the personal debris of the day in readiness for their trip to the illuminated service on La Montagnette: secular though they may be, they intend to seek calm in celebrating the assumption of the Virgin Mary at the Abbey of St Michel over at Frigolet. Various husbands and partners, having offered to drive, are relieved to learn that their services are not required: Louise will take Netty and Sophie in her flash car, whilst Phyllida conveys Madame Martin in a not-so-flash vehicle. Madame Lapin, having another type of fulfilment on her mind, is giving the outing a miss. By the time they all return, around ten o clock, the paella supper will be in full swing and the becalmed women will be able to close down this culmination of many months of planning in the tranquillity of a Provençal night.

Continuation

In the car park, they park the flash car, and the not so flash car away from the battered vehicles of the French who care little for bumps and scrapes. Christine takes particular care to avoid a small dusty red car that has clearly seen better days. Night has descended on Frigolet and we find our ladies sat behind Madame Berlioz in the atmospheric candlelight of the basilica. No-one can remember a time when this ageless and beautiful personage was not sat in the front pew during the service for the Assumption. Madame Berlioz dresses in the traditional style of Arlesienne women and retains an air of timelessness. She speaks with no-one and no-one approaches her, being, as they are, in awe. It's as if she's been purposely placed here in order that her presence can enrich the proceedings.

Our ladies of the night, along with the rest of the congregation, are in possession of their inverted triangular paper lamps in readiness for the procession. First, however, the clergy make their way to the altar accompanied by the choir's rendition of Salve Regina. Madame Berlioz maintains her elegant forward looking stance. Phyllida and Louise, along with Netty and Sophie, fumble their not-so-elegant troublesome way through the order of service. Madame Martin is simultaneously fumbling; not for her place in the service however, but for that sneaky little mobile phone which, these days and nights, accompanies her everywhere. From up on high, Mary tips her the spiritual wink.

The priest offers a short but comforting sermon regarding the visitation of Mary, unaware that she is personally visiting at least one of the congregated congregation as he speaks. And now it's time for the brothers to mingle with the crowds. They light the inverted triangles of those at the end of each pew. In turn, each person lights the lamp of those next to them until all the lamps are lit. Then, following the lead of the celibates, all exit the basilica and make their darkened way up and along the path to the statue of the Virgin at the summit. It's quite a crush. The crowds chant 'Chez Nous, Soyez Reine' to the accompaniment of collective emotion. In the midst of paneurythmic gymkhanas and uninvited cricket matches, something of the old way of doing things intercedes in the darkness of this place. Our ladies, tears in their eyes, are overcome by the unexpected meaning of the night and by life in general. But, in striving to be closer to Mary for a few minutes more, they lose their way amongst friends. No matter: they will find each other spiritually and prosaically later.

Under this best of Provençal skies, on the top of a small mountain, miles from anywhere, the service continues beneath the floodlit virgin. Phyllida is entranced. Half-heartedly, she looks around briefly in order to share the moment with her friends. By this time, many of the candles have waned and in the darkened throng, it's impossible to identify anyone she knows before the blessing is given and the crowd turns to descend the hill. She finds herself walking next to Madame Berlioz.

'Excuse me, have you seen my friends?' Madame Berlioz looks at Phyllida.

'Too late. Already gone,' she replies enigmatically before gliding onwards.

Back in the car park, Louise, Netty and Sophie sink into the extravagance of leather upholstery.

'Let's go', says Louise, 'I'm starving.' Other cars, including those that are red and battered, have already left the vicinity. By the time that Phyllida locates her car, having passed an inordinate amount of time trying to locate her friends, the car park is nearly empty. She assumes that Madame Martin must have journeyed home with the others. Phyllida spends about ten seconds thinking it might have been nice if someone had alerted her to this change of plan but forgives them all.

'Must've got tired of the crush,' she thinks and drives back to Cabannes.

Le Fin

In the field, chez Martin, the party is in full swing. Jean-Pierre Lucard is once again the paella prince supreme. The trestle tables are now occupied by all and sundry, revelling in this hot August night alongside the rosé and the best paella in the South – no time for cicadas, owls and singing frogs in this irreverent congregation. Team allegiances are discarded as are bats, balls, stumps and white clothing of all derivation. The winning score, however, is not so easily forgotten. At the make-shift bar, a throng has congregated in front of monsieurs les patrons of formerly opposing bars who are happily filling and refilling glasses.

Most of our protagonists are clustered at the end of a table, still congratulating themselves on the successful outcomes of two heady days when Phyllida arrives. She looks around but cannot see the person she's seeking.

'Where is Madame Martin?' she asks Louise.

'Why are you asking me?' comes the reply. 'She came back with you.'

'But I lost her,' Phyllida explains. 'And when I got back to the car park, everyone had gone. I assumed she'd come home with you.'

'What do you mean?' interrupts Monsieur Martin who has also been looking for his wife. 'Have you left her alone on La Montagnette?'

'It's impossible,' his now distressed neighbour responds. 'I'm telling you, there was no-one left there.' But now Phyllida, playing the last scene over in her mind, suddenly recalls something of importance. She whispers to Louise:

'Did you see an old red battered car?' she asks.

'No,' says Louise, 'it had gone before we left'.

Gradually, something that is not the following day dawns on the women. Something that is not the following day has not yet dawned on Monsieur Martin, but it won't be long. He, meanwhile, is distracted by Madame Lapin who has suddenly appeared clutching a piece of paper. It's a piece of paper she recently retrieved from an envelope she found in the bureau des affaires. The envelope has her name written on the front in very small writing that was composed by a tiny hand. Madame Lapin understands at the same time that she fails to understand how she has suddenly become the sole proprietor of a jam and pickle business.

And just as certain folk who are gathered at the end of a dusty lane that runs from the road between Noves and Cabannes are trying to make sense of what has happened, a huge harvest moon appears over the top of the pine trees in which the silent owls sit, and it sheds illumination on those below. Underneaththe trestle table, Clovis whines.

Madame Verte currently lives in Dorset where she also writes under the name of Alison Green. Read her blog about all things French and otherwise: http://donaldandtheweasels.wordpress.com/

17726602R00103

Printed in Poland
by Amazon Fulfillment
Poland Sp. z o.o., Wrocław